Remarque's L

Ben Joyner has no argument with the people who built their homes on the grassland near Pecos, but the cattlemen have long considered the range their own domain and now trouble is brewing. Rancher Gus Remarque is Ben's boss and believes that the dollar a day he pays buys not only a man's labour but his loyalty, too. The time is fast approaching when that loyalty might involve killing or being killed, and Ben wants to wash his hands of this dispute: he did his fighting during the war. So he quits the ranch and rides east without any intention of ever returning to that part of Texas. But a strong-willed woman and two would-be horse thieves alter his plans and he's back on the streets of Pecos when bullets begin to fly.

By the same author

The Hanging of Charlie Darke
The Drummond Brand
In the High Bitterroots
Return to Tatanka Crossing
A Storm in Montana
Longhorn Justice
Medicine Feather
Arkansas Bushwhackers
Jefferson's Saddle
Along the Tonto Rim
The Gambler and the Law
Lakota Justice
Crackaway's Quest
Riding the Line
To the Far Sierras
Black Hills Gold
Feud Along the Dearborn

Remarque's Law

Will DuRey

ROBERT HALE

First published in Great Britain 2018

ISBN 978-0-7198-2807-2

The Crowood Press
The Stable Block
Crowood Lane
Ramsbury
Marlborough
Wiltshire SN8 2HR

www.bhwesterns.com

Robert Hale is an imprint
of The Crowood Press

Typeset by
Derek Doyle & Associates, Shaw Heath
Printed and bound in Great Britain by
4Bind Ltd, Stevenage, SG1 2XT

PROLOGUE

Marty Levin had halted on a lump of land from where he could see across the slow moving herd to the river beyond. His face was set with unusual sternness and he barely acknowledged Ben Joyner's presence when the younger man pulled up alongside.

'Fixing to brew coffee here?' Ben asked.

'Not here.' Marty's reply was uttered barely above a hoarse whisper but it was clear that his decision was related neither to need for rest nor time of day.

'Never liked this place,' he said. He raised himself in his stirrups and set his eyes on a spot along the riverbank ahead. 'Fifteen years,' he muttered then turned to Ben. 'Fifteen years and the grass still doesn't grow properly.'

Ben, too, made himself as tall as possible in the saddle, attempting to see what Marty saw, but although his eyesight was keen, he detected nothing in the grass's colour or length that set it apart from the rest of the pasture. 'What happened?' he asked.

Marty removed his hat and wiped the sleeve of his shirt across his brow before speaking. 'This is where Mr Remarque caught those Mexican sheepherders. He hates sheep. Won't tolerate them on his land.'

Although this was the first time he'd heard of a conflict involving either shepherds or Mexicans, Ben wasn't surprised by the revelation. Being so close to the border, such confrontations had surely been inevitable, and his employer's attitude to sheep was no different to that of other cattlemen. The belief that sheep destroyed that grazing land which was the mainstay of their great herds marked them as another enemy to be repelled. Gus Remarque's rough justice in defence of his land had been at the core of many stories, which involved battles against Apache raids and tracking down rustlers who had tried to make off with his stock.

But currently there was a different tenor to Marty's voice. There was no hint that this tale would be embellished in the normal manner of bunkhouse bravado, indeed, there was no guarantee that Marty would expand on the few words he'd spoken. Ben figured it was the current situation that was raising bad memories in Marty's mind. Already that morning, the long-serving Long-R rider had indicated a tree from which two rustlers had been hanged shortly before Ben's arrival, as though he was reliving in his mind all the violence of the past.

Without a prompt, however, Marty spoke again. 'Killed them all,' he said, his voice a coarse rumble. 'Killed them and burned every carcass. Men, sheep and dogs. The fire smouldered for two days. Smoke spread across the river. Smell lingered for a week and the cattle still won't eat the re-grown grass.'

Ben surveyed the herd. He couldn't identify any stretch of land from which the cattle were shying away, but he figured that Marty's comment was more a transference of his own aversion to the place rather than a genuine observance of the behaviour of the animals in his care.

'Mr Remarque's a fair boss to those he employs; he's straight about what he expects for the money he pays. To others he's a stone wall and won't give an inch. I haven't always agreed with his decisions but I take his money so I don't go against him. But he was wrong that day, Ben. Those Mexicans had no intention of settling on this range. They were heading north where the grass is greener and lusher. If he'd left them alone they would have passed over his range within a couple of days. There was no reason to kill them the way he did, no need to slaughter all those animals.'

They sat for a few moments in silence, Ben mulling over Marty's story, knowing that he was stressing the fact that age wouldn't soften Mr Remarque's character.

Out of the blue, Marty asked, 'Thinking of quitting the Long-R?'

Ben nodded. 'It's on my mind.'

Marty's face twisted as though bothered by the sun. His eyes narrowed to thin slits but they remained fixed on Ben's face. He'd formed a high estimation of the young man's character and didn't want to be wrong. If he asked another question he might not like the answer, but the stopper was out of the bottle and it was necessary to examine the contents.

'Because of Mr Remarque's speech?'

Since the end of the War Between the States, the flow of immigrants from the east had increased and Texas was as eager to encourage settlers as every other state. Ex-soldiers of both armies, eager to find new homes for their families, were moving into the area. The land office in Fort Worth was specifying sections of open range available for settlement and newcomers were building homes and fencing off land that Gus Remarque had always deemed his own. For years he had defended it and wasn't prepared to lose it. The settlers must go. The previous evening, Gus had addressed his crew with words that proved his patience was at an end. The tactics he had used so far to dissuade the newcomers had had little success. Now he was prepared to adopt whatever measures were necessary to remove them and expected those he employed to carry out whatever instructions he issued. The crew had listened to and accepted the ranch owner's assertions with neither acclaim nor protest. He was their employer; accepting his dollar was an agreement to undertake whatever task he demanded. Herding cows or trampling down a neighbour's vegetable patch was all the same to them.

'I've been thinking of moving on for a while,' Ben replied. 'Thought I might give railroad building a try.'

There had been a lot of talk about the cross-continent railroad that was under construction.

'Heavy work,' observed Marty.

'Better pay,' Ben told him.

They both knew they were skirting the real issue. Ben said, 'Look, Marty, I did my fighting back east. I was one of the lucky ones: I survived four years of hell and didn't come west to take up arms again.'

Marty rubbed his jaw. 'Sometimes it's necessary,' he said.

'Sure it is,' Ben agreed, 'but I don't see this as one of those occasions. I don't have any cause to fight the people who are building homes along the river.'

'Mr Remarque says they are stealing his land,' Marty said. 'He's tried talking to them but they seem too stubborn to take his advice.'

'It's free range, Marty. They've filed on it. They've got papers from Fort Worth that back up their claim.'

Marty scoffed at that argument. 'People have come with papers in the past but Mr Remarque is still here.'

Ben guessed that that had been in the early days of statehood, when Mexico still insisted that the Nueces River was the border with the United States of America, not the more westerly Rio Grande. Aggrieved Mexicans had tried to regain land from which they had been forcibly dispossessed. Persistent claimants who weren't satisfied with Texan rebuttals of gruff incivility were repelled with gunfire. Many a Mexican who came seeking justice re-crossed the Rio Grande hanging over his own saddle.

'It might be different this time. These are Americans with deeds issued by our own government,' Ben argued. 'These people have legal documents, Marty.'

'Mr Remarque decides what's legal around here,' Marty said.

Gus Remarque's fierce attitude had established his authority in this area and he wasn't prepared to succumb to anyone who threatened it. As a consequence, no one was permitted to settle on his land. Anyone suspected of rustling was lynched without trial.

'Used to decide, Marty, but times are changing. Men who fought in the war aren't going to submit to any man's threats, no matter how powerful he believes himself to be.'

'You sound like you're siding with these settlers.'

'I'm not against them. I've talked to some of them. They're good men trying to do their best for their families.'

'Reckon you're talking about the big red-haired fellow.'

Ben Joyner squinted at the other rider. 'What's that supposed to mean?'

'Ah, come on, Ben,' Marty said, his tone half serious, half humorous, neither teasing nor sincere. 'I've seen you sparking with his daughter.'

Ben turned his head away, unwilling to betray his sentiments on the matter. Even though Marty was the person closest to being a friend on the Long-R, the war had taught him that friendships were liable to sudden cessation, so he never related his deepest thoughts to anyone. He shrugged dismissively, but knew that if he did leave this territory along the Pecos, Lottie Skivver would be the only person he'd rue leaving behind.

'What I'm saying is that it's time for me to move on. I never did intend pushing cows all my life and I have no taste for pushing honest people either. This isn't my fight.'

ONE

He could count on the fingers of one hand the number of people he'd spoken to since arriving in this one-street town, and they didn't include the woman crossing the street in the direction of the hotel whose porch he sat upon. Her business, he supposed, was with someone within the building, but her determined gaze was fixed on him as she advanced, her stride purposeful as though she had a quarrel to settle and no time to lose in doing so. She wore a wide-brimmed hat with a flat crown that protected her head from the growing heat of the day and shaded her eyes from the bright morning sun. Her upper body was covered in a red checked linen shirt accompanied by a plain blue scarf tied tightly around her neck. Black lace-up boots showed below the heavy hide skirt that reached from waist to calves. The city-style of her footwear was at odds with the less refined appearance of the rest of her apparel.

'Are you Joyner?' she asked, speaking before halting, as though the brashness of her approach would establish a position of superiority. The terse tone was matched by a facial expression of unremitting sternness, a proclamation that she would tolerate no obstruction to her purpose, whatever it might be. Ben figured she'd be a fearsome opponent if she had a gun strapped around her waist. As it was, he remembered his manners, rose to his feet and removed his high, grey hat.

'Yes, ma'am.'

'You've been in the chaparral country, out by the Pecos.'

Ben Joyner didn't know the source of the woman's information but couldn't deny its accuracy. 'Spent some time there,' he told her.

'Ever meet a man called Henry Tippett?'

'No, ma'am.'

'Think about it,' she ordered, as though the speed of his reply was a reflection of insincere thought rather than honest certitude. 'He's twenty-three now. A couple of inches below your height. Brown hair. Dark eyes.'

It was a description that fit a thousand men and she was as much aware of that fact as he was. 'He would be with an older man,' she continued. 'His uncle, Carlton Wellwin.'

'Sorry, ma'am.'

'Henry is my son,' she said, as though that might produce a different answer. 'Carlton's my brother.'

'Sorry, ma'am,' he said again. 'Can't say I've met either of them or heard anyone speak their names.'

Ben expected those words to put an end to the

encounter. He had no information to pass on, and therefore saw no reason for their conversation to continue. The woman, however, remained where she stood, her eyes fixed on his face as though expecting dogged resistance to shake from him the information she was seeking.

'Ma'am?' said Ben Joyner, prompting her to speak if she had more questions to ask.

'Stop calling me ma'am,' she snapped. 'My name is Elsa Tippett.'

'Is there something else I can do for you, Mrs Tippett?'

Her brown eyes flashed and her lips twisted, signs that the man's formality still gave rise to irritation, but she disguised the fact when she spoke again. 'Yes, there is. You can escort me to Pecos. I believe my son got that far. I want to find him, Mr Joyner, but I can't do it alone.'

Ben Joyner shook his head. 'You've set yourself an audacious task,' he told her, 'but I can't help you.'

'Of course you can,' she said. 'You've just come from that country. With your knowledge we'll be able to travel quickly. How many days has it taken you to get here?'

'Mrs Tippett,' he interrupted, trying to judge his next words, not wanting to give offence but keen to extricate himself from the woman's plans. 'Mrs Tippett, it wouldn't be proper for you and me to travel together.'

'Nonsense.'

'Mrs Tippett, you don't know anything about me.'

'Mr Joyner, issuing such a warning is testament to the fact that you are not a man I need to fear. Do you intend to rob me, Mr Joyner, or threaten me with harm? Are you a killer?'

For a moment, the memory of sighting along a rifle barrel filled his mind, along with images of distant men in grey tumbling as the weapon spewed out flame and smoke. 'Of course I don't mean you harm, Mrs Tippett, but such an arrangement could only cause damage to your reputation.'

'I'm a fifty-six-year-old widow who sacrificed reputation for survival a long time ago. If I'd allowed my life to be ruled by the prejudices of my neighbours, I would have never left Columbus, Ohio.'

'Mrs Tippett!' Ben Joyner's tone reflected his exasperation but she refused to acknowledge his attempted interruption.

'I came all this way with just Mr Raine for company and attracted neither harm nor scandal. I have no reason to expect that will be altered by travelling with you.'

Mr Raine was an unknown quantity to Ben Joyner. He neither knew Mr Raine's relationship with Mrs Tippett nor the manner in which they had travelled to this small town. No doubt train and stagecoach had figured large in their arrangements but those modes of transport were unavailable between this town and the Pecos River. There was neither the comfort of padded seats when on the move nor accommodation of the meanest kind at the end of the day. Long hours in the saddle were sufficiently torturous, but when united with meagre provisions and only hard ground for a bed they became conditions capable of dissuading tough men from ever leaving home again.

'Mr Raine came with you from Ohio?' asked Ben.

'St Louis,' she affirmed. 'We met in St Louis.'

'He came here with you?'

'He did, and he would have gone on with me if he hadn't fallen foul of a terrible accident.'

'He's injured?'

'He's dead. Tripped over a stray dog and fell under the wheels of a passing wagon. Killed instantly. So I'm in need of another travelling companion, someone who can guide me to Pecos.'

'I've just left there,' Ben said. 'I'm going in the opposite direction.'

Elsa Tippett drew back her shoulders. The accompanying intake of breath suggested she'd identified a flaw in Ben Joyner's character and that she was prepared to lower her own standards to accommodate him. 'I'm sure we can agree a suitable sum in recompense for your time,' she said.

Ben didn't reply instantly. The hesitation was caused by his need to find the right words to convince the woman that he didn't want to be involved in her scheme, but Elsa Tippett put a different interpretation on it. She was sure she'd found the chink in his armour and, with the application of a bit more pressure, would be able to buy his services.

'Do you have someplace to be?' she asked, her tone suggesting that she knew he'd drifted into town with neither a final destination in mind nor the prospect of employment in his immediate future. 'How far is it to Pecos?' She paused for only a moment before answering her own question. 'Four days? You can be back here in a week or ten days. I'll pay you fifty dollars for the delay.'

'I've been to Pecos,' he replied, the woman's persistence testing his temper. 'It's not my habit to retrace my steps. I'm sorry, Mrs Tippett, but you need to find someone else to take you through the scrubland.'

Ben Joyner replaced his hat and walked away, leaving the woman to burn holes in his back with her angry gaze. He headed for the livery barn at the far end of the street where he'd stabled his horse overnight. All the horses had been moved outside and the big chestnut was in a corral behind the stable with six other animals. It took only an instant to satisfy him that the horse had been well tended, not only with food and water but also with currycomb and wet cloth too. The ostler, a long, stooped fellow with a heavy limp, was washing a two-seat black buggy and, although he greeted Ben with a curt nod, he didn't allow his arrival to interrupt the work at first. After Ben had fussed his horse for a few moments, the stableman set aside his bucket and joined him, leaning against the poles of the corral.

'A fine animal,' he said. 'Haven't seen a better horse since leaving Kentucky in '58.'

Praise for the chestnut was welcomed by Ben; he'd valued it at sight and bought it from his employer's stock only days before beginning his journey. He ran a hand down the animal's long face.

'Saw the woman talking to you,' the stable man said. 'Offering to buy him?'

'Why would she do that?'

'Seemed mighty interested when she came to inspect him early this morning.'

Ben shook his head. Elsa Tippett was after him, not his horse.

'Brought the sheriff with her,' the stableman said quietly, throwing a sideways look at Ben. Unable to detect any kind of reaction, he asked, 'Will you be leaving today?'

It didn't escape Ben's notice that the stableman's tone was laced with the suspicion that the lawman's interest in the chestnut gelding might be cause for him to quit the town urgently. He was amused by the thought that he found facing Elsa Tippett again a more daunting proposition. 'Reckon I'll stay another day,' he told the stableman, then clapped the horse's neck before heading back up the street.

Ben Joyner's presence was a point of interest to the smattering of people to be seen on the boardwalks. Few spoke but he guessed that those who saw few fresh faces in their town had exchanged many nudges and comments. One man in particular caught Ben's attention. He was leaning against a stout post, smoking a black cigarillo and making no secret of the fact that Ben was under his scrutiny. He was a wiry character, long-legged and long-armed, which gave the impression that he lacked strength in his upper body. He wore a high, round-domed Texas hat that had neither dimples in the dome nor a rim sturdy enough to form side channels. If the man was fifty years old it seemed likely that the same hat had been clamped on his head for thirty of them. His shirt was grubby white calico and his blue trousers were rough denim. For Ben, however, the most prominent thing about him was the bright piece of tin pinned over his heart.

'I'm the owner of the chestnut down at the livery,' Ben said when he stopped alongside the lawman.

'Figured you were. I know everyone else in town.'

'Stableman told me you were interested in it.'

'Figured he would. Jake's never had the same control over his jaw as he has over horses.'

'So are you?'

'No. But Mrs Tippett now, that's a different matter.'

'What interest can my horse have for her? Why draw your attention to it?'

The sheriff shook his head. 'You've got that wrong, young fella. I saw the animal first. Check the stable every night when I patrol the town. I took Mrs Tippett to the stable this morning.'

'OK,' said Ben, beginning to weary of a conversation that seemed to be going nowhere, 'so what is so special about my horse?'

The lawman twisted his face with a grimace of amusement. 'Not your horse, exactly, but the brand burned into its rump.'

'What about it?'

'My book tells me that that is the Long-R mark of Gus Remarque.'

'It is,' Ben agreed, 'and I've got papers to prove I bought it fair and square.'

The sheriff's low chuckle was a disarming sound and his raised hands were a supplication for peace. 'I'm not accusing you of anything,' he said, 'I'm sure the beast is legally yours, but the Long-R is Pecos range and Mrs Tippett is trying to find someone to escort her there.'

'I've told her no,' Ben told him.

'Figured you had when I saw the storm in her face a few moments ago. She's come a long way to find her son. I guess your rebuff was hard for her to take. So close to her destination but unable to reach it.'

'Isn't there anyone in town who can take her?'

The man with the star shook his head. 'Not more than twenty-five men in this town who are eligible to undertake such a chore but none of them can go missing from their work for a week or more. In a small place like this every man is busy from dawn to dusk. Many have more than one job. I just pin this badge on when it's necessary. The rest of the time I'm the gunsmith and sometimes taxed with upholstering saddles and mending tack.'

Ben looked up and down the street trying to fathom why this spot had ever been chosen for a settlement. Judging from the well-weathered timbers, however, it seemed possible that some of the buildings were old enough to have been erected when this land still belonged to Mexico. The sites on which

Americans were given permission to settle by the Mexican government weren't always prime territory. Whatever had attracted those first pioneers to put down roots in this spot had apparently been strong enough for their descendants to remain after Texas gained independence.

'People usually stumble on this town by accident,' the sheriff told Ben. 'Travellers to and from the major cities tend to stick to the usual trails. We're too far south for Fort Worth and too far north for San Antonio.'

'But Mrs Tippett was travelling with a guide,' Ben stated. 'Was he lost when he brought her here?'

The sheriff shook his head. 'Raine claimed to know the area. A couple of years back, he'd worked cattle along the Mexican border. Reckoned that by quitting the main trails and crossing the scrubland they would reach Pecos more quickly. They'd be there now if he hadn't filled himself too full of that venomous brew that Sam Puddler calls whiskey.'

'Heard he tripped over a dog.'

'Dog's been accused, but there are witnesses who say that Raine was stumbling around so full of liquor that it would have been just as easy for him to trip over a splinter. Still,' he added ruefully, 'it means Mrs Tippett is stuck here until she can find someone to take her the rest of the way. No one can say when that will be and, even though Sam Puddler doesn't charge Houston prices for his rooms, she's likely to run out of money at some point.'

The implication that he should be the one to take

Mrs Tippett through the scrubland wasn't lost on Ben Joyner. 'Like I told Mrs Tippett, I'm going in the opposite direction,' he told the sheriff, but as he walked away he was nagged by thoughts of the woman's predicament. Whatever thoughts he had about the rashness of her undertaking, he wasn't blind to the courage and determination that had brought her this far, nor to the frustration that the delay must be imposing. However, there were two reasons why he was not prepared to assist her. One was a pledge never to return to the places he'd known. From coast to coast and north to south there would always be new land to cross and new sights to see. Never go back had become his golden rule.

Ben's other reason for staying clear of Pecos was wrapped up in his reason for leaving the Long-R spread. Times were changing, and homestead families were staking out sections of land earmarked by ranchers as part of their empires. Signs of conflict were growing and Ben had no taste for a range war. He had no property of his own and wasn't prepared to kill or be killed for land that belonged to someone else. He wasn't even convinced that the newcomers were in the wrong but he was sure that he didn't agree with the measures proposed by Mr Remarque. Damaging property and ruining crops had failed to scare away most of the newcomers and rumours had become rife around the ranch that the owner had sent for specialists to assist in the fight: gunmen hired to kill.

Nothing about that situation sat easily in Ben's

mind, so he'd quit his job on the Long-R ranch. The area was a powder keg waiting to blow. Pecos: a place for which he harboured no desire to return, and from which a lone traveller like Elsa Tippett should stay clear.

TWO

The men who arrived in town two hours later rode very slowly along the street. Being strangers was reason enough for them to attract the attention of the people on the boardwalk but the hobbling horse doubled their interest. Horses were revered in remote towns. Men's abilities were restricted without them, not only as a means of transport but also as an aid to his labours. As a result, it irked most citizens when an animal was misused or abused.

The rider was as lean as a willow sapling, his back straight and his chin jutted forward as though contemptuous of challenges from any man. His sunken cheeks were tanned dark brown, the colour of Navajos and Apaches, and that allusion was completed by the heavy brows and dark narrow eyes that flicked this way and that as he made progress through the town. Dust clung to his features, which were damp with sweat. His black hat sat low on his brow in order to cast a shadow over most of his face as protection from the burning sun. He wore a faded denim shirt and dark trousers that were tucked into black boots. His appearance was warlike and his demeanour hostile, accentuated by the ammunition belts that crossed around his waist and the ivory-handled Colts that filled each holster.

The second man was heavier, slouching and round-shouldered, as though he'd been in the saddle for several days. This, in fact, was true and every part of him ached from the jarring repercussions of the horse's persistent movement. His face was etched with surliness and fatigue but neither overshadowed the brutishness of his character.

The man sitting on the long bench of the rooming house wasn't deserving of anything more than a glance from them as they passed by, but they fell under his study. Ben Joyner had known men of similar ilk during the war. The heavier one had the face of a bully, someone who wallowed in savagery. The other was more cold-blooded, sadistic in his application of cruelty, a fact that was proven by his arrival on a distressed horse, knowing and enjoying the outrage it caused in this small community. It was an act that delivered a message with greater clarity than any words he could utter. He didn't tolerate opposition. He was a man to be feared.

They reined in outside the Dragoon, dismounted, and stepped up on to the boards outside that saloon. The tall one paused outside the swing doors before following his companion into the saloon. Slowly, he surveyed the street, as though daring anyone to criticise such behaviour: no man attended to his own thirst first when his horse was in greater need of attention. When no one met his gaze, he pushed aside the doors and went from the heat of the day into the darkened beer palace.

Across the street from where he sat, Ben saw the man who wore a tin star on his shirt leave his office. After a moment he crossed the dirt road to lean against the rail on which Ben had his feet.

'More people arriving in this town than ticks on a longhorn's hide,' he said.

'Just passing through, I suspect. No need yet to paint over the population count.'

'Guess not,' said the lawman. He rubbed his chin. 'Came in from the east, did they?'

It was a rhetorical question. He must have seen the newcomers pass his window, but Ben still told him he was right.

'Heading west then,' ruminated the other. 'Perhaps Pecos is their destination.'

Ben had come to the same conclusion. It wasn't one that he liked. The rumours he'd heard before quitting the Long-R filled his mind. The two who had gone into the Dragoon bore the hallmarks of the kind of men that Gus Remarque needed to clear away homesteaders. Hired killers. Instantly, the face of Lottie Skivver filled his imagination and he recalled the unexpected sadness he'd caught behind her smile of farewell the last time they'd been together. That had been in a Pecos storehouse; she with her parents gathering supplies and he gathering the paltry provisions needed for his journey.

Drew Skivver had expressed surprise when Ben informed the family that he was leaving the territory. 'Had you down for a man who would be keen to mark out his own 160-acre homestead,' the big, red-haired Pennsylvanian had said.

'Perhaps one day,' Ben had replied, 'when I've built a big enough bankroll.' In fact, the possibility of owning his own property had never occurred to him. He wasn't even sure that he was suited for farming or ranching, or perhaps he just didn't consider the land of the Pecos valley worth the fight that he knew was fast approaching. 'Take care, Drew,' he'd said. 'Gus Remarque doesn't want to part with an inch of land. He'll stop at nothing to drive you out of the territory.'

Finding it difficult to smile, Lottie had wished him luck. For a moment it seemed as though she had other things to say but she'd climbed onto the buckboard that was loaded with their purchases and it drove away. Ben had watched the family wending along the busy street hoping desperately that no harm befell them.

The lawman said, 'Reckon I'll have a word with those two. Find out how long they mean to stay in town.'

'Might want to tell them to get that horse unsaddled and tended to. It'll be lamed permanently if it's ridden again without treatment.'

The man with the star raised his hand in acknowledgement as he moved off towards the Dragoon. Ben regretted his words. Those men wouldn't welcome criticism, especially in a small town like this where the duties of the man with a star were mainly those of a recorder of events rather than an enforcer of law. There would be few instances of crime in a settlement of fewer than two hundred inhabitants. But to men like those who had just arrived in town, interference from such a representative of community law was likely to offer them an opportunity to leave their mark on the town. He knew their sort too well. In all probability they would humiliate the sheriff, perhaps kill him.

Ben's gloomy thoughts were swept aside a few moments later when the town marshal emerged from the Dragoon and headed up the street with a long, striding, rolling gait.

'Mrs Tippett still inside?' he asked Ben when he reached the rooming house.

There were few other places in town a visitor could be. Other than the Dragoon, which he'd just left, only the eating-house across the street and the general store were likely to have any appeal to visitors.

'I believe so,' Ben told him. More than once since their meeting that morning, Elsa Tippett had crossed his path and glared at him with undisguised anger but no further words had been exchanged. When the lawman went inside, Ben crossed the street and ordered a cup of coffee. If, as he suspected, the marshal had ascertained the destination of the two newcomers and dovetailed it with the need to get Elsa Tippett out of town, then it was a proposal that didn't sit easy with him. Although it wasn't his concern, he knew they were not men to be trusted. Any suggestion that the woman from Ohio was carrying a purse of fifty dollars or more was bait enough to persuade them to take her into the west and leave her body for the scavenger beasts of the wilderness.

From his seat by the window he watched as the marshal, accompanied by Elsa Tippett, returned to the distant saloon. The woman didn't enter but the two strangers emerged and all four engaged in conversation on the boardwalk. It was clear by their gestures that agreement had been reached although, when she stepped back onto the long, rooming house veranda, Elsa Tippett's features were not expressive of complete contentment. When she caught sight of Ben watching her through the eating-house window, however, she lifted her chin defiantly, proclaiming herself the victor of the situation before stepping indoors.

Ben had no reason to change his decision with regard to heading east. If his regard for Lottie Skivver hadn't prevented him leaving Pecos there was no reason why Elsa Tippett's need should get him to return there. Her quest, he told himself, had been foolhardy from the very beginning. Either her son would get in touch with her when he had found a home, or he was dead. It wasn't his concern if she was reckless enough to believe that a shared destination was sufficient justification to travel with strangers, yet he couldn't shake the belief that offering payment endangered her even more. He was angry that he was letting the woman's predicament linger in his mind and regretted his decision to stay in this town another day. Abruptly, he arose, crossed the street and announced to the rooming-house clerk that he was checking out.

With saddle-bags slung over his left shoulder and his rifle held in his right hand, Ben left the hotel and went up the street to the livery stable. The lame horse had gone from the hitching pole outside the Dragoon and Ben found it unsaddled inside the stable at the end of the street. Apart from that horse, the high, dark building was empty. All the other animals were outside in the corral where he'd run an eye over his gelding earlier that day. Voices floated to him from that direction and Jake, the stableman's, was curt with impatience and concern. Ben collected his saddle from the rail on which it had been set and carried it out through the rear the doors.

'The horse isn't mine to sell.' The tone of Jake's voice betrayed a change in the discussion. He was now less angry, more worried.

Although they had their backs to him, inspecting the horses in the corral, Ben had no difficulty in recognizing the two men who were the source of the stableman's consternation. The tall one, the one who had ridden in on a lame horse, was even slimmer than he'd seemed when astride a horse. If he'd been a critter brought in for the pot he'd have boiled down to nothing but bone and sinew. But he had a gun on each thigh, slung low like a showy gunfighter. He had a tight grip on Jake's arm, was shaking the older man as a minor demonstration of the violence he was prepared to inflict if the stableman refused to accede to whatever demand he'd made.

For the third person in the group, the burly man, Jake's nervousness was a source of amusement; the movement of his shoulders and head betrayed his eagerness to see the older man's abasement increased.

Jake tried to keep his voice steady when he spoke. 'I'm tending him for a customer. He'll be back for him soon.'

'I think you're lying,' the thin man said. 'You don't want to sell him to me.'

'He's not mine. I can't sell him.'

The tall man laughed but it wasn't a pleasant sound. 'I mean to have him,' he said. 'That big chestnut is just the horse for me.' He let his left hand slip to the butt of his six-gun. Then he grinned. 'OK. Don't sell him. I'll rent him from you. How much is one day's hire?'

Jake tried to shake loose from the man's grip. He stuttered when he tried to speak. 'N-N-Nothing. I can't. . . .'

'Nothing!' The man's voice held a jeering note of triumph. 'That's my kind of price. I'll agree to pay you nothing. Now,' he thrust Jake away from him, causing the liveryman to stumble and bang his head on the rails of the corral, 'saddle him up.'

Ben Joyner spoke slowly. His voice was low but carried authority and a menace that couldn't be ignored. 'That horse isn't going anywhere.'

The sigh that escaped Jake's lips could have been caused by surprise or relief, but there was no doubting the anxious look in his eye. The prospect of violence hung in the air like heavy snow on a winter bough and he was in danger of being engulfed by the oncoming downfall.

The tall man turned to face Wes. The leering grin that he had shown the ageing liveryman now turned into a scowl, angry that anyone would interrupt him at such a time. His irritation turned to scorn when he saw the figure before him. He knew his own ability with a gun and was confident that even in a fair fight he couldn't be outdrawn by the simple cowboy who stood before him, but, encumbered as he was with that saddle in his arms, he was no threat at all. Then he looked into the stranger's still, grey eyes and the first moment of doubt crept into his mind. 'Get outta here, mister. Don't mix in business that isn't your concern.'

'It is my concern. That horse is mine.' For a moment no one spoke. Even the animals in the corral were silent and motionless as though affected by the tension of the moment. Eventually Ben spoke again. 'If you've got some business here, just get it done then move out. I don't want to see you in this stable again.' Ben was very still, his legs slightly apart, as though secured to the ground. Yet there was no illusion of tension in the stance. His face, too, showed neither humour nor anger, nor any sign of fear. He just waited for the man to move. Only his eyes carried any kind of threat: not once had he blinked. His gaze had fixed on the face of the tall man from the moment he'd stepped outside the stable and hadn't strayed for an instant.

'You think you can give me orders?' The tall man wasn't accustomed to being spoken to in such a manner. When ultimatums occurred in his conversations they were usually issued by him. He regarded the man again, and again allowed his confidence to be boosted by the fact that his opponent's hands were full of saddle. His own hovered over his gun butts. 'You think you can back up your words?'

Ben nodded slowly. Jake tried to shrink his body so that it was hidden by one of the narrow corral posts. The tall man went for his guns. Wes dropped the saddle. While talking, he'd adjusted it so that most of its weight had been in his left hand. Unseen by the tall man, Ben's right hand had been holding the stock of his rifle. Before the saddle hit the floor and before the man had cleared leather the rifle was grasped firmly and menacingly in Wes's hands. He pointed it first at the tall man then at his companion, making it clear to both that he had the upper hand, that he could kill them if they didn't obey his instructions.

'Slowly,' he told them, 'unbuckle those belts and let them fall to the ground, then step away from them.'

While he kept them covered, Jake collected and unloaded the weapons before hanging them in their holsters over the top rail of the corral.

'Came in with a lame horse,' Jake explained.

'Wanted to replace it with your chestnut.'

'Have you got anything more suitable, something that won't leave you out of pocket?'

'Reckon so.'

Jake brought a dun mare out of the corral. Ben kept his gun on the tall man while he fixed his saddle on its back. When they were mounted, Ben threw the pair their gun belts. 'Ride,' he told them. 'Don't come back. If I see you near my horse again I'll kill you.'

The scowls that had appeared on the faces of both of his adversaries when they'd found themselves faced with Ben's cocked rifle were still in evidence when they rode away from the stable. Without looking back they rode swiftly out of town, but not until they were distant specks did Ben relax his finger on the trigger.

'Reckon I got the best of that deal,' Jake said, the accompanying rough chuckle meant to disguise the nervousness he'd experienced only moments earlier. 'When that horse of his is fit again it'll be worth a lot more than the one he rode out of here.'

'Compensation for the rough treatment,' Ben suggested.

'And the cost of stabling and treatment until it can earn its keep.'

Ben propped his rifle against the rails of the corral, running his eye over his chestnut as it mingled with the other animals. It looked well rested, ready to carry him away from this small town, but before he could bring it out of the enclosure his attention was captured by a shout from the building behind him.

The sheriff stepped out of the stable. 'Where did those men go?' he asked.

'West,' Ben told him.

'They'd agreed to take Mrs Tippett with them.'

'They didn't have time to wait for her.'

'What do you mean?' asked the man with the badge.

'I told them they had to get out of town. Fast.'

'Why?'

'Because there was a chance I would have killed them if they'd hung around here any longer.'

'Wanted to take his horse.' It was Jake who supplied that information, and added, 'Would have done, too, if he hadn't turned up when he did.'

'But Mrs Tippett,' the lawman said, 'she was depending on them to get her to Pecos.'

Ben's grimace expressed his opinion of that plan; there was barely any need for the words he spoke. 'Mrs Tippett wouldn't have got ten miles into the wilderness before they took her money and killed her. Men like that travel fast; they wouldn't want anyone tagging along that would encumber their progress. Tell Mrs Tippett to be sure of the honesty of the next person she tries to hire.'

'Tell me yourself,' said Elsa Tippett who, having witnessed the departure of the men she had hoped to escort her on the last stage of her journey, had followed the lawman when he'd hurried up the street to the livery stable.

'Mrs Tippett,' Ben began, but she wouldn't let him finish.

'I don't care to hear your opinion of their character. Those men were prepared to guide me to Pecos and I was prepared to travel with them and take any associated risk. You've driven them away and left me stranded in this town once more. You owe me, Mr Joyner. You owe me your time and your protection until I reach Pecos.'

Ben Joyner's reservations regarding the hardship of the journey and the dangers she was likely to encounter, not only en route but also when she reached the Pecos territory, were dismissed by Elsa Tippett. She understood the risks, she told him, and was prepared to face them. She was packed and ready to leave and if no one was prepared to accompany her on the trail west then she would go alone.

Ben wasn't sure that he believed her declared intention; he reckoned the threat was merely a feint to weaken his resolve, but when he spoke against such a course of action he could hear the first tones of submission in his voice. Although he disclaimed any debt was due to her for ridding the town of the two men who had tried to steal his horse, he still possessed a natural inclination to assist those in need of help. His reluctance to accompany her would have been overcome easily if they had been travelling in the same direction. As it was, returning to Pecos would involve rejecting the diktats of his own philosophy, but the woman's persistence eroded his opposition gradually, and in the face of the attending lawman's efforts on the woman's behalf, Ben eventually agreed to escort her to Pecos.

Elsa Tippett wanted to leave instantly but Ben insisted on delaying their departure for twenty-four hours.

'Those men were making tracks for Pecos,' he said. 'It wouldn't be in our interest to meet up with them out in the scrubland.'

So Ben returned his saddle to the rack in the stable and re-took the hotel room he'd vacated recently.

THREE

Sam Puddler slopped a measure of whiskey into the shot glass and pushed it across the counter to Ben Joyner. 'Safe journey,' he said.

Ben raised an eyebrow. 'I didn't expect my departure to cause any kind of a stir around here.'

The bar owner had a wry smile on his face. 'Every event, no matter how insignificant, causes a stir around here.'

'Did the sheriff spread word that I'm quitting town tomorrow?'

'Don't rightly matter who spread the word,' Sam said. 'Truth of the matter is that it's the departure of your travelling companion that's aroused most interest.'

'Oh!'

Sam Puddler chuckled. 'Don't get me wrong, everyone here likes Mrs Tippett.'

'But?'

'But she's burned the ears of every man in this town ever since Brad Raine fell under the wheels of

Tad Vaughan's wagon. She's a determined woman.'

'Don't I know it?'

'Got some fixation in her head, the fulfilling of which is likely to drive a man crazy. Just hope it's not you.'

'But you don't really care as long as I get her out of town.'

Sam Puddler's laugh was good-natured. 'Swallow your drink and I'll fill you up again. Then hope that the haze lasts four days until you reach Pecos.'

Ben recalled the sheriff calling Sam Puddler's whiskey a venomous brew and when he tipped the glassful into his mouth he had no cause for argument. He refused a refill, opting instead for a glass of beer, which he carried to a table where a penny poker game was in progress. He won a few hands and lost a few more before quitting the saloon, his mind fixed on the route he would take back across the wasteland towards the Pecos River.

Darkness had fallen. Ben paused on the raised boardwalk allowing his eyes to become accustomed to the change of light. The air was cool and beyond the walls of Sam Puddler's saloon the silence was like a confining vacuum. The moon was hidden by clouds and the street was unlit; not even the crudest form of public lighting had been adopted by the town. The blackness of the night was only disturbed here and there by a window glowing yellow from an inner lamp. The hotel was one of the buildings that could be identified in this manner but Ben turned away, sauntering in the opposite direction. Despite the lateness of the hour, sleep wasn't upon him and he suspected it wouldn't come easily this night. Although he was resigned to the task of escorting Elsa Tippett, the reluctance remained. He couldn't shake off the belief that he'd been trapped into performing the errand. Although he had no pressing need to be anywhere else, his reason for quitting the Pecos country was still pertinent. He'd washed his hands of the trouble that was brewing there and had no wish to risk involvement by returning.

Ben reached his destination, the stable at the end of the street. Although he had no reason to doubt that his horse was fit and ready to travel the following day, he knew that a few minutes of his company would provide it with reassurance that it had not been forsaken. A cowboy and his horse were partners. Soft snuffling sounds came to him as he made his way along the side of the building to the rear corrals. He figured that some of the horses had picked up hints of his presence – not alarmed, merely communicating with each other. He wondered if the chestnut had recognized his scent because he doubted even a cat's ability to recognize him by sight in such deep darkness. When he reached the corral he climbed on to the bottom rail. It took only a moment to realize that only three animals were within the enclosure, their dark forms shuffling slowly, moving away from his watching place in cautious unison. The chestnut was not one of the trio. Even in darkness it was apparent that none of the corralled animals had either the stature or bearing of his big horse.

He turned his attention to the building behind. His horse, he supposed, was occupying one of the inner stalls. As he approached the big rear door he could see that it was slightly ajar. The interior was dark but a small lamp burned somewhere towards the front of the building. Its light was dim, not strong enough to reach the doorway through which Ben had entered.

'Jake,' he said, his voice conversational so that he didn't startle the stableman or wake him if he was dozing.

The only response came from a beast occupying one of the stalls deep within the stable. Its neigh was high-pitched as though the animal had been unnerved by the intrusion of a human voice. Momentarily, Ben was bewildered by that reaction because he'd recognized the sound of his own chestnut. Elsewhere in the stable, another horse moved, its ironclad hoof striking the timber of its stall. Up ahead, where the lamp's low light glimmered, a movement caught Ben's attention. He stepped forward, Jake's name again on his lips, but before he was able to utter the word his foot came into contact with an object on the ground and he stumbled forward, pitching full length onto the floor. The supposition that his fall had been caused by a saddle or another piece of equipment was soon driven from his mind. Whatever his foot had struck had not moved an inch; the texture resembled more that of a sack of animal feed or vegetables. Such untidiness seemed out of keeping with the diligence he'd observed in Jake's usual practise around the stable. He called again for the stableman as he scrambled on to his knees.

Footsteps hurried towards him through the darkness. A shape loomed over him and, although he knew that darkness could play tricks with the mind, he knew instantly that the man reaching down wasn't Jake. This was a burly man who, when he'd taken a handful of Ben's shirt, was able to pull him up with greater ease than that of which the old man would have been capable. Instinct prepared Ben for the punch that was driven against his midriff. No words had been uttered prior to the attack but the man's silence provided as much warning of his intentions as a blood-curdling cry from an Apache brave would have done.

The punch was meant to drive the air out of Ben's body but, guessing his assailant's intent, he'd twisted to the right. Although it missed its target, the blow caused damage and pain, crashing as it did into the ribs below his heart. He grunted, tried to grab the other's arm to prevent another blow but received a push that sent him staggering into the hard timber frame of the stall behind. The animal within snorted its displeasure but Ben was more concerned by the animal without who was approaching with violent intent. His foe was bulky but his arms moved quickly and the fists on the end were capable of inflicting a great deal of damage.

Again, Ben moved to his right, gambling that the

other favoured punching with his right arm and his first swing would come from the left. In the darkness, however, it was impossible to be sure, he couldn't see the man's face clearly enough to read any signs it might betray. Indeed, when the blow was delivered, it almost caught Ben unaware. It wasn't the expected looping haymaker but a straight right that glanced the jaw below Ben's left ear. In response, he drove a punch of his own deep into the other's belly. His adversary grunted and gasped as the air left his body and the left hand swing that had been the follow-up to his straight right dropped across Ben's shoulders after passing harmlessly behind his head.

Ben threw another punch, slamming his fist against his opponent's chest above his heart. The man cursed. It was at that moment that Ben realized his assailant was not alone. He was urged on by a voice from behind.

'Finish it, Gatt. Quickly. Let's get out of here.'

Ben had put behind him the surprise he'd received at the onset of the affray and knew that the handicap of darkness applied as much to his opponent as it did to himself. Although he was outweighed by his foe, his confidence had begun to grow in his ability to see off the attack. A second man, however, was a setback and, whoever they were, the odds of success were greatly in their favour. Ben could discern Gatt's shadowy movement as the bigger man shook off the effect of the blow he'd taken and lurched forward to engage in the brawl once more. Ben, too, advanced, getting close to his adversary, hoping to make it impossible for him to deliver punches with a full swing of his arms. They grappled, hauled at each other, each trying to find an opening in his opponent's defence, each grunting and cursing with the effort they were expending in their struggle for domination.

For an instant, the man called Gatt thought he'd gained the upper hand. With an upward swipe of his right hand he knocked aside Ben's grip on his shirt and was in a position to hurl his opponent away from him, thereby providing room to swing a punch that, if successful, would put an end to the fight. Ben, however, reacted quickly. While maintaining his grip on Gatt's shirt he kicked out, his hard-toed boot connecting painfully with the other's knee. Gatt yelled and stumbled. Ben rammed his head into the other's chest, driving him backwards with clumsy steps and the obstacle that felled Ben when he first entered the stable now had the same effect on Gatt. He went over, landed on his back with Ben, whose shirt he still gripped, atop of him.

Gatt's associate, anxious lest the noise of the fight and the unrest it had caused among the stabled animals should bring their presence to the attention of other townsmen, now became involved in the scuffle. He withdrew his gun and used it as a club against Ben's head. Fortunately for Ben, the darkness combined with his vigorous attempt to overcome Gatt made it impossible for the third man to get a clear strike. Even though the blow wasn't hard enough to incapacitate Ben completely, he was stunned momentarily. Amid his wooziness he heard his new assailant urge Gatt to flee the scene. He could also hear a horse being led reluctantly from the stable, its neighs and rears unsettling the other animals.

As Ben struggled to his feet, the men were quitting the stable through those doors that led to the rear corral, leading the horse that continued to lodge a protest. Once again he recognized the sound of his own animal and followed the horse stealers outside. The heavy clouds had shifted in the sky and the moon was high and full above the town. The light it provided was minimal but seemed brilliant in comparison to the dense blackness inside the stable.

Ben paused in the doorway. He could see his assailants making their way along the side of the corral. 'That's my horse,' he yelled into the night, knowing they wouldn't stop, that the words were wasted, but he wasn't going to allow anyone to steal his horse.

A gunshot cracked in the night and a bullet thudded into the stout wood door by which Ben was standing. He drew his revolver, not willing to shoot in case he hit the chestnut, but he was determined that the men who had attacked him and stolen his horse would not escape.

Across the corral, Jarvis Wilson cursed his companion. 'Hurry,' he ordered. 'That gunshot will arouse the whole town, Gatt.'

Ben ran from the doorway to the corral rails. One of the thick posts provided cover while he attempted to discern the activity of his enemies. When it was clear that they had moved beyond the corral, he set off in pursuit. Although it was necessary for them to cross thirty yards of open terrain to reach it, it soon became clear that their immediate goal was the solitary low oak tree on the edge of town. Movement under the tree caught his eye and he wondered if accomplices were waiting there to provide cover while they made their escape. He advanced more cautiously until he was certain that the saddles of the two horses waiting under the tree were empty.

From the buildings of the settlement arose the sound of voices – citizens curious about the gunshot, Ben supposed, but too far distant to be any help in his effort to foil the act of horse stealing. If it was to be prevented then he had to act alone. The men had reached the tree and were trying to gain their saddles, but the one who had charge of the chestnut was not having an easy time. The big horse continued to pull on the long lead rein, reluctant to go with the unknown men.

Ben shouted again, then took a risk. He didn't want any harm to come to the chestnut but only bullets would stop the thieves' flight. He waited, knowing that when they were mounted they would present higher targets; he would be able to shoot over the chestnut's head. If he missed they would escape and he would have lost his horse.

When they were in the saddle he took aim. One of the men saw him and fired but the bullet flew wide of the mark. He returned fire: one shot at the burly man who was holding the lead rein of the chestnut. He saw the man slump forward, then his right hand released the lead rein in order to clamp it against his left shoulder. Ben fired again, by which time townsmen were rushing towards him to investigate the hullabaloo. The would-be thieves rode away but the chestnut went nowhere, bowed its head to graze on the coarse grass and waited for Ben to guide it back to the stable.

Jake the stableman had been the obstruction on the floor responsible for twice bringing down Ben Joyner. When he was able, he confirmed Ben's suspicion by identifying the men as the two that had been chased out of town earlier that day.

'Reckon they want your horse real bad,' he said, while someone bathed away the blood he'd lost when they'd pistol-whipped him.

The lawman who was conducting an inquiry into the disturbance regarded Ben with no little concern. 'I'm pleased you're leaving town tomorrow,' he declared.

FOUR

Elsa Tippett was impatient to set out but Ben Joyner refused to leave the settlement until the sun was two hours beyond noon. Although certain that his attackers wouldn't renew their efforts to steal his horse, he was still wary of an encounter with them in the desolate country that stretched almost to the Pecos River. One of them, the bully called Gatt, had stopped one of his slugs so they wouldn't be travelling fast. It was fixed in Ben's mind to be extra vigilant on the trail: he would insist upon making camp if he saw dust or smoke ahead.

When Elsa joined him outside the hotel she was wearing a short jacket over a blue shirt and leather trousers that were tucked into calf-high boots. She flashed a look at him from under the wide brim of her flat-crowned hat that bespoke her irritation better than any words she could muster. It was a look that promised bleak companionship for the next four or five days. Ben watched as she tied well-filled saddlebags behind her saddle. He hoped the contents weren't all women's doodads, that she'd had the gumption to pack some provisions for their journey, too. She also had a rifle, which she slid into the boot that would be clamped by her right leg when she mounted the mare.

'Can you work one of those?' he asked.

'It belonged to Mr Raine. He said it was foolish to travel in these parts without the means of protection. So I brought it along.'

'But can you use it?'

'I know you point it then pull the trigger,' she answered.

Ben grunted, wishing, even at this late hour, for a reprieve from the task in hand, but none came. Resolved to getting Elsa Tippett to Pecos as quickly as possible, he climbed into the saddle. 'Let's ride,' he said, and turned his horse to the west.

The sheriff, leaning against a post outside his office, tipped his hat as they passed and Sam Puddler, standing outside the Dragoon, sent them on their way with a promise to Ben that the beer would still be cold when he returned. Ben barely acknowledged the whiskey seller's remark; he'd already decided he'd give this place a wide berth after delivering Mrs Tippett to Pecos. Even though he was in the process of breaking his own mantra never to go back to a place he'd known, there was no reason to abandon it forever. Besides, his short stay in this settlement hadn't been good for him; there was nothing about it that justified a second visit.

The remainder of the daylight hours passed pretty much in the air of silent testiness that Ben had anticipated. He wasn't troubled by the lack of communication: he looked upon the journey as a job not dissimilar to herding cows from one range to another. Men got on with their tasks during the day and jawed and swapped stories when they gathered around the night fires. He set the pace, sometimes covering a half-dozen miles at a steady, loping run before slowing to a dust-dragging canter or walk. Elsa Tippett remained a length behind the whole way, matching his changes of pace without question or complaint. They saw no other travellers and covered more than thirty miles before Ben decided it had become too dark to travel. There was nothing special about the place he chose for their camp because the semi-arid territory was unchanging for more than a hundred miles.

'I'll tend to the horses while you gather up some sticks and brushwood,' he told the woman.

By the time she'd gathered an armful of fuel Ben had hauled the saddles from their mounts, tethered them and allowed them to lap water from his hat.

When he set about building a fire he told Elsa Tippett that they wouldn't be cooking food. 'We'll use some of the water from our canteens to brew coffee,' he told her 'but we'll leave the bacon and beans until the morning. The smell of frying bacon will attract coyotes. We don't want to be troubled by them while we're trying to sleep.'

Elsa Tippett kept her own counsel but the look she

threw at Ben seemed to convey a suspicion that he was being unnecessarily Spartan. He retrieved some hardtack biscuits from his saddlebags and gave a couple to his companion. She eyed them as though they were the meagre rations for a despised prisoner. Her distaste eased a grin out of Ben.

'They're fresh,' he said, and bit into one as though proving the point. 'During the war,' he added, 'the ones they issued were so old that we had to drop them into hot coffee before we could eat them.' When Elsa's eyes flickered with a glimmer of interest, he supplied the reason for the soaking. 'Full of insects. Weevils, mainly. The boiling coffee killed them and they'd come floating to the top. We had to skim them off before drinking.' He laughed, remembering the deprivations endured even by a victorious army.

'Blue or grey?' Elsa Tippett asked, the question dismissing as insignificant the wartime fodder of a soldier, the colour of his uniform being a more important consideration.

'Does it matter?'

'My son fought for the Union. My brother, too. I just wondered if their conditions were equally bad.'

Ben wasn't sure that that was the real purpose of her question, but the war was three long years past and it was time for those divisions to be healed. 'Made no difference, Mrs Tippett. Everyone who fought was issued with tainted provisions, even the officers.' He paused before speaking again and supplied the answer she really wanted. 'Blue, Mrs

Tippett. I wore a blue uniform.'

She nodded, as though that answer had some deeper significance, then bit into the biscuit.

'When did you last see your son?'

' '63, when he went off with the 33rd Ohio Volunteer Infantry.'

'He didn't return home at the end of the war?'

'No. Him and Carlton had plans to settle out here. The free west, they called it.'

Ben had known many men in the ranks with similar dreams, but for everyone who followed them through he figured there were dozens who hadn't. 'When did you last hear from your son?'

'I got Henry's last letter in '67.'

'Two years ago!'

'The letter came from Fort Worth, full of hope that they'd found the right place to build a home where I'd be able to join them.'

'Two years,' Ben repeated, the thought clanging in his head that such a lapse of time most probably meant that her son and brother were dead.

'Mr Raine had information that they'd moved to the region around Pecos,' the woman was saying, her voice projecting certitude in her mission. 'I expect they've established a home somewhere along the river.'

'And if they haven't, what do you do then?'

'Why are you so sceptical, Mr Joyner? Why shouldn't I find my son in Pecos?'

'You haven't heard from him for two years. Surely you've considered the possibility that he never reached Pecos?'

A flash of determination – or perhaps it was accusation – filled her eyes when she next addressed Ben Joyner. 'Are you telling me he's dead? That someone killed him? Why would you think such a thing?'

'I didn't mean to imply that someone killed him, but he could be dead. Accidents happen, illnesses, too, and men get lost and perish without water in this scrubland.'

'I don't believe that,' she declared, 'and I mean to keep going until we reach Pecos.'

'I've promised to get you there, Mrs Tippett, and I will, but I won't be hanging around that town for more than a day, and I think you need to have some plan for a return east in case your family can't be found.'

There had been a moment in their conversation when a thaw in their relationship had seemed possible, not to the point of friendship but at least warm enough to make their time together in the ensuing days bearable. But Elsa Tippett told Ben that she had no intention of returning to Ohio, unfurled her bedroll at the other side of the fire and lay down to sleep with her back to him.

While he was frying bacon the following morning, Elsa Tippett approached Ben.

'How long did you work at the Long-R?' she asked.

'Close on two years.'

'And you never met Mr Raine?'

'Can't say that I did, but I heard some talk of a Bud

Raine who'd quit the place before I got there. Could be the same person.'

'Last night,' she said, 'that talk about my son being dead. . . . Was that meant to persuade me to turn back?'

Ben shook his head. 'Returning to the Pecos territory wasn't in my plans, Mrs Tippett. I don't want to do it, but I said I would and I'll see the journey through.'

Those words seemed to satisfy the woman. She stretched out a hand that was holding a small leather pouch. 'There's fifty dollars in there,' she told him.

'I don't want your money, Mrs Tippett. Never did. I'm doing this to release me from any obligation you think I owe you. No other reason, but you're on your own when I get you there.'

He scooped the bacon onto two plates, which already contained hardtack biscuits and a shared tin of beans, and they ate in silence.

When they rode away, Elsa Tippett kept her horse alongside Ben's. Little was said but, in Ben's opinion, the atmosphere between them was less brittle, as though he'd been tested and adjudged honourable without knowing of what was considered unworthy. In keeping with the previous day, Ben set the pace, but he was considerate of Elsa's unfamiliarity with long horse rides and broke the journey whenever she needed to rest. They camped that night in a gulch, through which water ran. Their replenished canteens would last until they reached Pecos.

The remains of a recent fire suggested to Ben that

the would-be horse thieves, too, had used this place, and a bloody rag lying close by seemed to confirm his suspicions. From the heat that was still in the embers he estimated that the pair had stopped here around midday, putting them four or five hours ahead. Perhaps more if they were travelling fast to get Gatt to a doctor. But they came across no other signs of those men or any other until the last morning when they were within a few miles of the Pecos River.

By this time they had left behind the rough land of grit and cacti and were crossing the greener pastures of the Pecos valley, which fed the cattle herds of the Long-R and other ranches. Even so, the wagon that was on track to cross their route half a mile ahead was travelling so fast that it was kicking dust high into the sky. As they drew closer to each other, Ben could hear the crack of a whip being snapped over the heads of the straining team and could make out the stocky figure of a man in a blue shirt bent to his task. The wagon was almost past Ben before he recognized the driver.

Dick Garde was one of the six or seven men who had marked out a homestead along the river north of Pecos. His eyes were fixed on Ben as he yelled his urgency at the horses. Ben raised a hand in greeting but its intended friendliness was nullified by the expression on Dick's face. The scowl was indicative of the existence of a deep-rooted argument, but there had never been a cross word between them. Bewildered, Ben watched as the flat wagon rumbled past. It was then that he saw the figure lying in the back, pitching and rolling with every jerk and twist resulting from the vehicle's rapid progress. The man was barely conscious, his clothes were torn and grubby and his face was battered and bloody from brow to chin. Ben might not have recognized him if it hadn't been for the red hair atop his head. It was Dick Garde's neighbour, Drew Skivver.

Concerned for his friend and curious to know how Drew had sustained the injuries, Ben shouted for Dick to halt the wagon. At first, he thought he hadn't been heard above the pounding hoof-beats and the ringing of the iron-rimmed wheels on the hard ground, but when he dug his heels into his horse's flanks and set off in pursuit it became clear that no thought of halting the team existed in Dick Garde's mind. Instead, when he looked back and realized that Ben was intent upon pursuit, he cracked the whip repeatedly, demanding greater effort from the horses.

Ben couldn't account for the homesteader's determination to put distance between them; he had done nothing to arouse the man's enmity. However, he couldn't deny that there had been something accusatory in the scowl that had been aimed at him when passing, a suggestion that he bore some responsibility for Drew Skivver's injuries. He reined to a halt: it seemed clear to him that by continuing his pursuit he would only increase Dick's anger. Scratching his head in puzzlement, he looked back over his shoulder to where Mrs Tippett watched and waited for him to re-join her. Whatever burr was under Dick Garde's saddle would have to remain there until he'd got her to town.

It was necessary to cross the River Pecos to gain the town that carried the same name. Although the river was neither wide nor deep at this point, a bridge had long ago been built to accommodate the passage of wagons and livestock. After crossing it, Ben Joyner and Elsa Tippett made their way through the scattering of riverside adobe buildings that remained of the early Mexican settlement before reaching the timber frame buildings of American construction. Austin Street, the longest thoroughfare, had become the centre of the community, and the Alamo Hotel, which occupied a centre block, was their destination. It was reputed to be the best hotel between Fort Worth and Chihuahua, which meant a room there would cost Mrs Tippett a good deal more than she'd paid to stay in Sam Puddler's rooming house. If it were more expensive than her finances permitted then she would have to seek out alternative accommodation after he'd quit the town. He'd brought her to Pecos, but he was obliged to do nothing more for her.

On entering Austin Street, they could see men spilling out of Shay Dubbin's saloon and gathering in an ever-quietening semi-circle around its corner entrance until a heavy, awkward silence hung over them. An argument had been brought outside and every non-participant was anxious to see the outcome. Conversations were non-existent; men wanted only the evidence of their own eyes and if they had an opinion on the rights or wrongs of the argument they were keeping it to themselves. Their mood had attracted the attention of passers-by and tradesmen in the vicinity, and all commerce had come to a standstill. Ben Joyner and Elsa Tippett, too, reined their animals to a halt, their way ahead hampered by the street throng.

On the raised boardwalk outside Dubbin's Saloon, the antagonists faced each other. At first they numbered four and Ben was able to put names to three of them. Two of them, Arnie Arentoft and Frank Faulds, had staked claims north of town alongside Drew Skivver and Dick Garde. Arnie's round face, so often beaming with good humour, was red with an anger that also coloured his raised voice. His English was good but he had never lost the accent of his home country. People called him the Dutchman, which he didn't object to.

'I bought my land,' he announced. 'Frank, too,' he added, flinging an arm in his companion's direction, making it clear to everyone they had legal entitlement to the stretch of ground on which they'd built their homes. 'Everyone along the river can produce deeds that will be upheld by the law.' He looked around, not only to harness the support of his fellow settler but also, it seemed, in the expectation of finding a lawman at his side who would corroborate his words.

It was the third man that Ben knew who answered.

Davey Pursur was foreman at the Long-R ranch. 'That's grazing land and you have to go. Mr Remarque has tried to be generous but your stubbornness is trying his patience.'

'Generous!' the word explode from the Dutchman's mouth in a shower of spittle, which he wiped from his long, fair moustache with his thick forearm. 'Mr Remarque has had our crops trampled, our homes attacked and our women-folk and children frightened by his riders. Those are the actions of a coward and you can tell Mr Remarque that we will not move on just because he is displeased with our presence.' He ended his speech with a curt nod, an affirmation that he would stand by his words.

'Then I suggest you move on because your presence sickens me.' The speaker was the fourth man on the boardwalk, the one who was unknown to Ben Joyner. He pushed Davey Pursur aside so that he was standing almost toe-to-toe with Arnie Arentoft.

Some of the colour left the Dutchman's face but he wasn't prepared to step away from this man's threats any more than from those made by Gus Remarque. 'What you did to Drew Skivver was the work of an animal, but you couldn't have done it alone. You needed four men to hold him while you whipped him.'

Frank Faulds tugged at the Dutchman's sleeve. Arnie hadn't been in town to witness the beating that Drew Skivver had taken; he'd only heard an account of it from Frank. Frank was worried that he hadn't sufficiently stressed the brutality of the beating that had been dished out to Drew and certainly didn't want to watch it being repeated. Arnie shook him off.

'Do you think you are strong enough to beat me on your own?'

The man with Davey Pursur grinned. 'I don't have to.' The batwing doors were swept aside and more men stepped out of the saloon and ranged along the wall behind the speaker. Ben Joyner recognized some of them as Long-R riders. Marty Levin was among them. 'However,' the man continued, 'you're carrying a gun and you've called me out so I guess that means I've got to face you man to man.'

Frank Faulds tried once more to extricate his friend from the calamity into which he'd talked himself. 'Come away, Arnie.'

Again Arnie Arentoft disengaged himself from the other's grip, although this time it was a more reluctant manoeuvre. He knew he couldn't win a gunfight with this man or any other. 'Step away, Frank,' he said.

A grin spread across the face of the man facing Arnie. 'Just go,' he said. 'Let everyone in town know just who the coward is here. And when you get home, pack your belongings and get clear out of the territory.'

'The land is mine,' Arnie uttered quietly but with grim determination.

'Then go for your gun.'

It all happened so quickly that no one could really confirm that the Dutchman had made any move to draw his pistol. What was certain was that it never cleared leather. Three bullets struck his upper body before he slumped to the ground and another smacked into his forehead while he lay spread-eagled on the street.

With a dismissive grunt, the man led the Long-R riders back into the saloon and Frank Faulds removed his hat as he stood over his friend's body. Ben Joyner glanced at his companion.

'You warned me,' she said, then gigged her horse forward towards the rail outside the Alamo Hotel.

FIVE

From his bedroom window, Ben Joyner had watched men load the Dutchman's body onto a flat wagon. Frank Faulds had driven it out of town in much the same way that Drew Skivver had been taken home by Dick Garde. Drew's wife, he hoped, would be able to nurse her husband back onto his feet, but Anya Arentoft would have to bury hers.

Now, Ben could see Sheriff John Vasey in conversation with one of his deputies. Both men seemed puzzled, as though at a loss to know why they were on the street outside Shay Dubbin's saloon or what they were supposed to do now that they were there. John Vasey was scratching the back of his head in such a manner that it had tipped his sombrero forward to sit low on his brow. At one moment, the deputy was looking along the street towards the river, then the next in the opposite direction, past the Alamo Hotel, as though the resolution to his dilemma was about to ride in from Mexico, or the Long-R ranch, which was closer. The sheriff's duty seemed clear to Ben; enter the saloon and arrest the man who had slain the settler. Everyone who had witnessed the fight knew that Arnie had been goaded into the deadly affair, that reaching for a gun was as alien to him as farming corn was to a Cheyenne warrior. He cursed, knowing it was impossible to prove the man guilty of an offence. Every Long-R rider would testify that both men had gone for their guns, which, by the law of the west, made it a fair fight. Arnie's killer would go unpunished. Grabbing his hat, Ben quit his room. He'd been in the saddle for four days but was unable to rest, his brain too active for his body to seek repose.

Although the dispute between the Long-R and the settlers was not his concern, he was unable to pass the lawmen without questioning their intentions. He got the response he expected, that enquiries had led the sheriff to believe that there was no case to answer.

'The killer used Mr Remarque's name with freedom,' Ben observed. 'Who is he?'

'Col Brodie. Thought you would know that. Don't you ride for the Long-R?'

'Not anymore. Quit almost two weeks ago. Is he a hired gun?'

' A cattle-pusher. Came in from New Orleans a few days ago.'

'Yeah,' Ben murmured, 'New Orleans teems with cattle. Reckon you'd better keep an eye open for another pair of experienced cattle-pushers who probably arrived here yesterday. I don't know their names but one is slim and mean and the other one is carrying a lump of my lead somewhere about his body.'

The sheriff and deputy exchanged a look but didn't speak. Ben filled the gap with words. 'They tried to steal my horse, twice. I reckon they're here because Mr Remarque is willing to use any means at his disposal to wipe the settlers out of this territory.'

'Mr Remarque is a powerful man in these parts but I expect him to operate within the law.'

'Within the law as he sees it, Sheriff.'

'You sound like a man who means to stand against him.'

Ben paused a moment, remembered that he'd completed the task that had brought him back to Pecos, and then shook his head. 'I won't be around long enough to do that.'

'Then I suggest you leave me to attend to the law in Pecos.'

'That's fine with me, but just be sure whose law you're attending to: Mr Remarque's or the State of Texas.'

As Ben turned away, he caught a movement at the batwing doors of Shay Dubbin's saloon. Someone turned their head away as though anxious not to be caught watching, receding until swallowed by the darkness of the beer palace's interior. Without conviction, Ben thought it might have been Marty Levin, but his curiosity wasn't sufficiently spiked to warrant him following the man inside. Besides, there would be talk in there about the shooting of Arnie Arentoft and glasses raised in toast by some of the men on the Long-R payroll. Ben didn't regard it as a cause for celebration. Instead he climbed onto the chestnut and rode out of town, back across the bridge and northward to the stretch along the Pecos where the families had built their homes.

Ben had mistaken the identity of the man who had overlooked his conversation with the lawmen. Gatt Stone made his way from the batwing doors to the table at the side of the long bar where Jarvis Wilson was in conversation with the foreman of the Long-R. Although eager to acquaint his partner with the information he carried, Gatt's progress was necessarily slow. With his arm in a sling and a roomful of men who had taken aboard too much whiskey to be considerate of his injury, it was his own responsibility to guard against accidental collisions that had the ability to engulf him with pain.

Following the fight with Drew Skivver, Sheriff Vasey had told Davey Pursur to take his men back to the ranch, but that advice had been ignored. They had descended upon Shay Dubbin's saloon and remained there ever since. They were in high spirits. Their boss would be pleased; every strike against the settlers secured his grip on the territory. Davey Pursur had even hinted at a bonus for those who had been involved in the attack on the red-haired landgrabber if their tough tactics proved to be enough to chase the settlers away from their holdings along the Pecos River. The killing of the Dutchman by Col Brodie, he reckoned, was probably the blow that would achieve that goal. Such was the gist of his conversation with the thin-faced Jarvis Wilson when Gatt reached their table.

'Your special services might not be required,' Davey Pursur was saying. 'I doubt if these farmer types will have the backbone to remain around here now that the talking has come to an end.'

'Well, we're here now,' drawled Wilson. 'Your boss still has to pay what he promised.' He looked up, caught the expression on Gatt's face and waited for his companion to approach.

'Our friend with the horse is here,' Gatt said. 'He's out on the street talking with the sheriff.'

Wilson pushed back his seat and, ignoring the question thrown at him by the foreman, rose swiftly and crossed the room. Like Gatt, he didn't go outside. Instead he paused at the side of the batwing doors and peered into the street. At first, he could see neither the sheriff nor the man who had been instrumental in twice forcing him out of the small town that lay across the scrubland. The man who was also responsible for putting a bullet in Gatt's shoulder and who had deprived him of owning the finest animal he'd seen for several years. He turned his head and looked down the street towards the bridge across the river, but without reward. Although there were several people going about their business along the sidewalks, the man he sought was not among them.

Shifting his position he was able to look up the street and his eyes picked out the sheriff by his curious gait as he made his way back along the street to his office. Of the man whose life he wanted to take, there was no sign.

'Are you sure it was him?' Wilson asked Gatt when the shorter man reached his shoulder.

'Certain.'

'Then I'm sure we'll meet again soon. You'll get revenge for that hole in your shoulder and I'll get a new horse.'

Drew Skivver's place bordered a creek of the Pecos where, from the rise of ground where Ben looked down on it, it seemed as though a great scoop of land had been removed to leave a fertile, basin-like pasture that was ideal for a small homestead. The Skivver family had been in the territory for less than two years but already a collection of timber buildings had been constructed, a clear statement of their determination to remain. A stone chimney dominated one wall of the house, and from it, smoke was rising in a long grey line into the sky above. Ben nudged his horse forward, moving slowly down the incline, looking for signs of activity about the place. He couldn't see anyone in the yard but counted a number of horses that, he figured, belonged to neighbours who, like him, had come to learn the extent of Drew's injuries. Their presence lifted a slight worry from Ben's mind; it was late in the day for unexpected visitors and, if they'd been alone, his arrival might have alarmed Lottie and her mother.

He was thirty yards from the house when two riders emerged from a small copse of cottonwoods and willows. They were riding fast as though racing to the house with an urgent message. Ben pulled on the reins, halted the chestnut so as not to impede the progress of the oncoming riders. He thought he recognized one as the son of Dick Garde but he didn't get a good look at him, nor did he have time to study his companion. Suddenly, as they got closer to Ben, it became apparent that the object of their ride was not to reach the house but to attack him. Both riders were armed, one with a rifle, the other with a stout stick with which he began instantly to belabour Ben. Clearly, his intention was to crack open Ben's head, but by twisting and ducking the blows landed on his arms and shoulders. So ferocious was the assault that Ben had little opportunity to voice his protest, nor could he reach for his gun knowing that a rifle was aligned on him and that given any opportunity the armed man was likely to blow him out of the saddle.

In order to avoid a clumsy swing of the club, Ben twisted his upper body, thereby presenting his back to his assailant. Taking advantage of the situation, the attacker jabbed the stick roughly into Ben's back, a blow that was not only painful but also unbalanced him, so that when he was struck in that place a second time, he fell to the ground. He was given little time to regain his equilibrium but when his attacker dismounted to continue the pummelling, Ben lunged at his legs and brought him crashing to the ground under the legs of the horses. Ben scrambled onto his knees, delivered a punch that landed with some force, but which he had no time to celebrate. A rifle butt was smashed against his head and he slumped, stunned, on to the ground.

Barely conscious, Ben could offer little resistance. Any small struggle of which he was capable was answered with kicks and punches. A rope was wrapped around his body, pinning his arms to his side, and the men used it to drag him to the gateway that led into the yard of the Skivver settlement. He was hauled upright and another rope coiled around him in order to tie him to a fencepost. One of his assailants began shouting, hailing the house to arouse those inside.

The fuzziness of his thinking slowly clearing, Ben tried to form a protest at his treatment but the barrel of a rifle was pressed against his abdomen.

'Keep up the fight,' a voice said, 'and I'll willingly pull the trigger.'

'I haven't done anything,' Ben replied.

'Come spying around here for Gus Remarque,' accused his captor, 'and you can expect the same sort of treatment that was meted out to the Dutchman.'

Ben recognized Jonas Petterfield's husky voice but other noises began to reach him as other men hurried across the yard to investigate the hullabaloo caused by the upraised voice of Dick Garde's son. It was Dick Garde himself who was first to reach the fence.

'What's going on here?' he asked.

'Caught him sneaking up on the house. Come to spy for the Long-R,' Jonas Petterfield announced, once more poking the end of his rifle with bruising ferocity into Ben's stomach.

Ben grunted. 'Quit doing that,' he said. 'I didn't come here to spy on anyone.'

Dick Garde came closer, peered into Ben's face. 'You ride for the Long-R,' he said.

Ben shook his head in denial. 'I don't,' he said, wincing as he began to feel the effect the pummelling had had on his body.

'Sure you do. I recognized you when you tried to ambush me earlier.'

'I wasn't trying to ambush you.'

'Sure you were. You and another man were waiting to finish off Drew Skivver outside town.'

'You've got it wrong,' Ben said.

Another man brushed Dick Garde aside to get a closer look at their prisoner. Frank Faulds nodded his head as though confirming his own thoughts. 'He rides for the Long-R, sure enough, and he was on the street when Brodie gunned down Arnie.'

'What are you doing here?' Dick Garde wanted to know. 'Have you come with an ultimatum from Gus Remarque or were you fixing to find out the purpose of our meeting?'

'I don't have any argument with anyone settling in this area. I quit the Long-R two weeks ago. Drew's a friend. I wanted to know what happened to him, how serious his injuries are.'

Someone scoffed at the suggestion of friendship.

'It's true,' Ben insisted.

'I suppose your partner is also a friend of Drew's,' Dick Garde retorted. 'Which raises the question of his current whereabouts. Waiting for you beyond the ridge, I suppose.'

Enquiring looks were directed towards Dick's son and the other rider who had captured Ben, but they were sure that Ben had been alone.

'You'll find her in the Alamo Hotel. She has no involvement in your dispute with the cattlemen.'

A momentary stillness settled on the group around the fencepost, confused as to their reaction to Ben's claim that his earlier companion had been a woman. Current events had made them suspicious of the words and intentions of everyone outside their small circle of families; consequently, any unexpected announcement needed time for consideration. In the lull, another figure, hurrying across the yard from the farmhouse, joined the group.

'What's happening?' asked Lottie Skivver.

'We've caught a spy,' said Dick Garde's son.

Lottie's eyes fell on the figure tied to the post but she dismissed the young lad's words when she became aware of the identity of the bound man. 'Ben,' she said. Immediately, she took in his rumpled and grubby clothing and the marks of conflict that showed on his face. A line of blood ran from the corner of his left eye to his mouth, the result of the blow from the butt of his assailant's rifle. 'Untie him,' she ordered.

'He's one of Remarque's men,' said Frank Faulds. 'We need to know what he's doing here.'

Lottie reached for the rope and tried to undo the knot. 'I thought you'd gone away,' she said to Ben.

'I did.'

'What brought you back?'

'It's a long story.'

Frustrated by her inability to work the knot loose, Lottie asked someone to cut the rope.

'We don't know why he's here,' Dick Garde protested.

'I don't work for Gus Remarque,' Ben snapped. 'I didn't know you were holding a meeting here. I came to find out what's happened during the days I've been away and the extent of Drew's injuries.'

Jonas Petterfield, whose acquaintance with Ben in the past had, like that of the Skivver family, been amicable, stepped forward and sliced through the rope. It was only when he was released from his bindings that Ben realized that he was still suffering from the blow to his head. The dizziness caused him to stumble but he didn't fall. Raising his hand to his brow, he discovered the sticky line of blood.

'Come up to the house,' Lottie said, 'and I'll bathe that wound.'

Unable to investigate the disturbance in the yard, Drew Skivver anxiously awaited the return of his neighbours. In addition to the multitude of bruises and cuts he'd suffered during the attack on him in Pecos, his right arm had been broken and at least one rib had been fractured, too. His wife, who sat at his side, had packed pillows and blankets around him, both for comfort and to prop him up so that he was able to participate in the meeting that had been arranged hastily. Because he hadn't been fit enough to travel, his home had been chosen as a meeting place to discuss the settlers' response to the violence that had been unleashed against them. For no reason he could explain, finding the face of Ben Joyner amidst those of his neighbours gave rise to optimism, that the trials they were currently suffering would be resolved without further trouble.

A seat was placed close to Drew Skivver and Ben put into it. Lottie tended to his injuries while he exchanged details of the previous few days. Although an element of suspicion with regard to his purpose for being in the vicinity still lingered in the minds of Dick Garde and Frank Faulds, his character was vouched for by Drew Skivver and Jonas Petterfield and the other men were swayed to believe that he had no evil intent.

'Five men turned up at Frank's place a week ago,' Jonas told Ben, stretching out an arm to make it clear that he was talking about Frank Faulds. 'Told him to get out of the territory. Burned a barn, killed three pigs, broke down fences and spoiled a garden of vegetables.'

'Frightened my wife and the boys,' Frank supplied. 'Pointed their guns at me like they were going to shoot me down and next time they probably will. Meg, my wife, wants to pack up and leave. I don't.'

'Then there was a fight in Dubbin's saloon a couple of days ago. That was the first time any of us had seen Col Brodie. He picked a fight with Joe Shelby like he did with Arnie Arentoft today. Joe wouldn't draw his gun.'

'I wasn't carrying a gun,' interrupted Joe Shelby.

'So he fired at his feet, chased him down the street with the whole town watching.'

'And you, Drew,' Ben asked, 'was it Brodie who did that to you?'

It hadn't been. Col Brodie hadn't been in Pecos when Drew had encountered Davey Pursur and some of the Long-R crew. Heated words had been exchanged, which had led to a fight that he couldn't win.

'Don't suppose I would have got out of town alive if Brodie had been involved.'

'What about Sheriff Vasey? What is he doing about the situation?'

'He's Remarque's man,' Dick Garde said. 'He's not going to change.'

'It was Vasey who put an end to the attack on me,' said Drew.

'And we're thankful for that,' said his wife.

Lottie, having quelled the flow of blood from her patient's face, inspected it for any minor cuts or scrapes that required attention. Her eyes met Ben's and for a brief moment the expression of concern that had dominated her feelings since first coming across him tied to the fencepost, relaxed and she smiled at him. 'You'll survive,' she said.

Dick Garde's rough voice put an end to their amiability. 'He did nothing to prevent the killing of the Dutchman,' he said, referring to Sheriff Vasey's absence from the street when shooting had occurred outside Dubbin's saloon.

'What are your plans now?' Ben wanted to know.

'We're staying,' declared Dick Garde. 'We'll defend our properties. No one is chasing me away.'

'They've proved they're prepared to kill to get what they want. Are you sure you're prepared to risk the lives of your wives and children?' Ben saw the darkness of anger pass across Dick Garde's features and knew he was thinking that his first intuition had been correct: Ben had come to spread consternation among the settlers at the behest of Gus Remarque. Ben raised his hand in supplication. 'Don't get me wrong,' he said, 'I'm not trying to interfere with your decision; just want to be sure that you understand the situation. Col Brodie is a hired gun. He'll be itching to earn his pay and gather any bonuses he's been promised.'

The room fell quiet; they all understood that the bonus payments would be in lieu of bodies and destroyed homesteads.

Dick Garde said, 'We'll face whatever Gus Remarque throws at us. If we stand together we can overcome one gunslinger.'

Those words were greeted with brave murmurs of approval and Ben knew that his response would again make Dick Garde suspicious of whose side he was on. 'I don't think Col Brodie is the only gunman that Gus Remarque has brought to Pecos. I ran into two men who were heading this way in a scrubland town four days ago. They tried to steal my horse. One of them is a tall, slim fellow and the other is more squat and hefty. I put a bullet in one of the pair.'

Frank Faulds shuffled his feet. 'I've seen them,' he said. 'They were in Dubbin's saloon when Arnie and I went in for a drink.'

'Which one did I hit?' Ben asked.

'The shorter one. The one called Gatt Stone. His right arm's in a sling.' Secretly, Ben would have preferred it if he'd put the other man out of commission; he suspected that the tall man was the more dangerous gunman. 'The other man's called Jarvis Wilson. Are you looking for them?'

Ben shook his head. 'If they stay away from me and my horse then I'll stay clear of them.'

'What brought you back here?' Drew Skivver asked.

'It's a long story,' he said, 'but scaring off that pair sort of obligated me to act as a guide to a woman who wanted to come here.'

Lottie Skivver tried not to show interest in the fact that Ben had returned to Pecos in the company of another woman but Dick Garde had no such qualms. It was information that concurred with what Ben had told them earlier and even if the cowboy's reception by every member of the Skivver family hadn't been so cordial, the truth of a woman companion was enough to put an end to any lingering belief that their earlier meeting had been part of a plan to ambush and kill Drew Skivver.

'Her name's Elsa Tippett,' Ben announced. 'She's trying to find her son and her brother. She was told they were heading in this direction but hasn't heard anything from them for two years.'

'That's about the time we all came out here,' said Jonas Petterfield. 'Tippett,' he muttered, playing with the name as though somewhere in the deep reaches of his mind there was a memory that was linked to it.

'Henry Tippett!' It was Lottie who spoke the name.

'The Ohio Kid,' her father said, managing a smile for his daughter, sharing a memory with her.

'Yeah, and his Uncle Carl,' Jonas Petterfield added, recollection of their names affording him some pleasure. 'They left Fort Worth a couple of weeks before the rest of us. We expected to meet up with them here but we never saw them again. Perhaps they changed their destination after leaving Fort Worth, or perhaps some disaster befell them, but they weren't here when we staked out our claims. We asked around but no one had any knowledge of them.'

Although it wasn't good news, it was something to pass on to Mrs Tippett. He figured she would want to speak to anyone who had known her son and brother. His suggestion that they make themselves known to her when they were next in Pecos was met with an uncomfortable silence.

'We mean to form a group to undertake any future visits to Pecos and they will be for essential supplies only,' Dick Garde told him. 'No one will be hanging around that town longer than is necessary. We ought to be able to avoid trouble if we get there early morning while the Long-R riders are still on the range.'

The nods that accompanied Dick Garde's words proved to Ben that this was one of the strategies that had been agreed prior to his arrival. If these men were scared by the violence that had been meted they weren't showing it, nor could he detect any reluctance to defend the land on which they'd built their homes. No one raised an objection to him bringing Mrs Tippett out to their homes, so he collected his hat and prepared to leave. He sensed that they would prefer to reconvene their meeting without him in attendance.

Lottie walked outside with Ben when he went to collect his horse. 'Perhaps you and your parents should stay with another family for a while,' he said.

'We're not leaving here.' Her tone was adamant. 'If we abandon this place for any length of time, Gus Remarque's men will burn it to the ground. You know that. I'm surprised you would even make such a suggestion.'

'If you come under attack, how will you defend yourselves?'

'My father is strong enough.'

'Not at the moment. He's an invalid and no matter how determined he is to protect you and your mother, he can't do it against killers when his arm is broken.' In the gathering gloom he cast a look around the homestead. 'Some of your fences need to be repaired,' he said, 'and other points around the perimeter need to be strengthened. Your father isn't capable of doing that.'

Following his glances with studied looks of her

own, she allowed only a moment of silence before answering. 'I'll do it.'

Ben knew that any defence lines that the settlers were able to put around their homes would probably be insufficient to deter or repel any determined attack. It was apparent that Gus Remarque was prepared to do whatever was necessary to achieve his aim of clearing out the settlers. Ben knew that he couldn't abandon the Skivver family while they faced the threat of an attack by armed and unscrupulous men. 'If you'll let me, I'll come back tomorrow to help.'

'Do you mean to stay in Pecos?'

Ben didn't know what his plans were. 'At least long enough to mend your fences,' he told her.

SIX

The last of the crew were attending to their equipment while listening to Davey Pursur, who was issuing their orders for the day. When horse harnesses had been checked and chaps had been secured, they mounted up and rode off to tend to their allotted tasks. Before they were through the gate, the foreman turned his attention to the ranch house that stood fifty yards inside the compound. Minutes earlier, he'd seen and been surprised by the figure standing on the veranda. He couldn't remember the last time the boss had been outdoors before the sun had fully cleared the horizon. Davey Pursur surmised that Gus Remarque was perked by yesterday's events, cheered by those incidents that would surely guarantee victory over the settlers and deter all opposition to the cattleman's rights. Even though the current homesteaders had staked their claims along the river on the far side of Pecos, they couldn't be allowed to settle. If they became established in the area, others would follow and spread onto the best land for feeding the Long-R herds. He crossed the compound, calling a hearty greeting to the ranch owner.

Gus Remarque sniffed the fresh morning air as he stood on the ranch house veranda. It had become his usual practice after breakfast to attend to correspondence and office matters, but this morning he'd risen from the table, come outdoors and revelled in the sounds of men and horses preparing for the working day. It brought home to him the achievements of his life, the battles he'd fought and won to claim this land, and the risks he'd run and successes he'd had that had placed him at the pinnacle of power in this region. The limitations of this land for grazing beef, even the hardy longhorns, were obvious for all to see. Across the river, where the beginning of the Chihuahua Desert was only a stone's throw away, it was impossible for cattle to survive. Only by good management had he been able to maintain and increase his herd, forever moving them around the eastern scrubland for whatever nourishment it could provide, but needing the more lush grass along the river's fertile strips to fatten them for market. He couldn't afford to lose an acre of pastureland and, no matter what papers were written in Fort Worth, he had no intention of doing so.

Although his views were shared by the other cattlemen in the region, he was aware that they were more cautious in their handling of the problem. So Gus had decided that it was his lot to lead the way, knowing that every interloper he successfully chased away from the river valley would encourage the other ranchers to follow his example. Between them they would keep the grassland open for their grazing herds.

'Where's Brodie?'

'He stayed in Pecos with the new men you hired.'

'I want to see him. Get someone to bring him here.'

'He said he was coming to see you. Wanting his bonus for killing the Dutchman, I guess.'

Gus Remarque fixed his steely grey eyes on his foreman. It was none of his business what arrangements had been made with the *pistoleros* and he was about to tell him so, but Davey Pursur was the first to speak.

'Don't know why you didn't leave the job to me and the boys. We've always handled trouble in the past.'

'There hasn't been trouble like this in the past,' Gus Remarque told him. 'This is bigger than anything I've had to deal with and I need men to do it that, when the chips are down, aren't going to decide that shooting and being shot isn't what they signed up for.'

Davey Pursur defended the men. 'You've got a good crew here, Mr Remarque. They won't let you down.'

'One man quit before anything developed,' he replied. 'I don't want others doing the same. Their job is to herd cattle. Besides, when this is over and Brodie and the other men I've brought in have finished their job, the rest of us still have to live around here, still have to visit Pecos. It'll be easier for them if they've played no part in the conflict.'

'Bit late for that, Mr Remarque. Our men have already raided the homesteads and destroyed barns and crops.'

'That phase is at an end. I've got professional men on the payroll now whose job it will be to clear the settlers from their homes.'

'Don't know how effective they'll be,' said the foreman.

'What's that remark supposed to mean?' snapped his boss.

'One of the pair who arrived in Pecos yesterday has his gun arm in a sling. The doctor had to dig a slug out of his shoulder when he got to town.'

Gus Remarque glowered. He'd decided to put an end to the threat that settlements along the river posed to his herd and he'd offered top dollar to the men he'd hired to push the job through to its conclusion. He wasn't pleased by the information imparted by his foreman. Wilson and Stone had agreed to his terms so had no business becoming involved in any affray that jeopardized the success of the job he'd hired them to do. He had no intention of paying doctor's bills or expenses for inactivity while they nursed wounds they'd suffered pursuing their own arguments. 'If he's not up to the job I'll get someone else who can do it,' he said, adding, 'I'm not paying good money for failure.'

His boss's words had begun to rile the foreman.

'Hope you won't forget that it was me and the boys who attended to Drew Skivver yesterday. He's the one the other settlers listen to. They'll follow his example. If he goes they'll go with him, and if he goes because of the beating he took yesterday then any bonus is due to me and the boys, not Brodie.'

'Speak to me like that again and you won't even be drawing pay,' Gus Remarque snapped at him. 'I decide who gets what. Nobody else.' He turned to go back into the house. 'Send Brodie to me the moment he gets here,' he said over his shoulder.

It was almost an hour since Ben Joyner had eaten and he was sitting in the foyer of the Alamo reading a five-day-old San Antonio newspaper when Elsa Tippett descended the broad stairway. He allowed her time to order breakfast before following her into the hotel's dining room. She received the news that he had found people who had known her son in Fort Worth with less eagerness than he had expected, but he imagined that that was due to the weariness of the journey they'd recently completed. The information he was capable of imparting was slight but she agreed to ride out to the Skivver farm to speak with Lottie and anyone else that had knowledge to share. First, though, she needed time to eat breakfast.

Ben had left the chestnut in the stable attached to the hotel but instead of saddling the animal he hired a buggy that was available and had the groom harness one of the hotel's horses to it. It was late morning, later than had been his intention, when he reached the farm with Elsa Tippett beside him. Lottie was in the yard, her face red with effort and smudged with grime, testimony to the fact that she'd been busy tackling the repairs and reinforcements that Ben had promised he'd attend to the previous night.

'I thought you'd decided not to hang around,' she said as she opened the gate for him to drive the buggy through.

Ben couldn't blame Lottie for the fact that her greeting was less than warm. If circumstances had been different, if Drew Skivver hadn't been incapacitated as a result of the attack on him by the Long-R crew and if Arnie Arentoft hadn't been shot dead outside Shay Dubbin's saloon, he would already be far from Pecos, trying to resume the journey he'd begun before crossing trails with Elsa Tippett. But he hadn't gone, even though the reason for hanging around Pecos wasn't clear in his mind. Two weeks earlier, when there had been little more than a threat of trouble between cowmen and settlers, he'd had no qualms about riding away, but now, with the spillage of blood, turning his back on the situation carried a taint of cowardice. Almost involuntarily, and despite the hired guns that had been brought in by his former employer, Ben found himself favouring the cause of the region's newcomers. Although he'd fought in the war, he knew he wasn't a match for the professional quick draw *pistoleros* and had no reason to believe that his presence would add any real fire-power to their cause, but he couldn't desert them, especially the Skivvers, who were virtually defenceless. Their neighbours might be keen to help them but their hands were already full protecting their own properties.

'I brought Mrs Tippett,' he said. 'It seemed a good opportunity to introduce her to someone who'd met her son.'

The women exchanged smiles and Ben ushered them into the house, with assurances for Lottie that as soon as he'd un-harnessed the horse from the buggy he would take over the tasks that needed doing to strengthen the farm's defences.

Jonas Petterfield rode up to the Skivver farm in the early afternoon. He had come to assess the extent of Drew's recovery after a night's rest and to undertake any tasks that were proving too difficult for Lottie and her mother. Finding Ben Joyner already at work in the yard surprised him but heartened him, too. It meant that the absence from his own farm wouldn't be as lengthy as he'd envisaged. Still, when Ben set aside his hammer and pail of nails and joined him at the water butt that stood in the shade at the side of the house, he tried to keep his surprise hidden.

'What brings you out here?' he asked.

Ben wondered if he was still under suspicion, if the accusation that he was a spy for the Long-R had prompted the question. 'I brought Mrs Tippett out to learn whatever she could about her son and brother. Figured I'd give Lottie a helping hand while I'm here.'

'Throwing in your lot with us?'

'Trying not to pick sides.'

'You intending to hang around Pecos?'

'I'm not sure.'

'Well, if you do, you won't be able to sit in the middle of the storm that's coming. There aren't many smallholdings in the territory at present but none of us intend to surrender our land. We're here and we're staying.'

'Mr Remarque needs the grass for his herd to survive.' Ben didn't know why he'd put forward the cattleman's point of view even though he'd spoken the truth. Gus Remarque's needs weren't the issue; it was the violence he was prepared to unleash upon law-abiding citizens that Ben was opposed to.

Jonas Petterfield fixed him with an intent stare. 'Well,' he said eventually, 'if you stay you'll have decide where you stand. Things have gone too far to avert conflict.' He turned away and began to move towards the house door.

'You can tell Mrs Tippett I'll be through here in an hour.'

'You're not staying here at the farm?'

Ben understood Jonas Petterfield's concern. With a broken arm, Drew was virtually incapable of protecting his family if Gus Remarque launched an attack. 'I've got to get Mrs Tippett back to Pecos,' he said. It was a reply that was as unsatisfactory to Jonas as it was to himself.

Lottie Skivver was in conversation with Jonas when he left the farmhouse at the end of his visit. They talked earnestly until Jonas climbed into the saddle. Out of the corner of his eye, Ben could see both of them casting glances in his direction but he kept at his task until Jonas rode away. Lottie closed the gate then crossed the yard to join Ben.

'Almost finished,' he told her and took a look around at the results of his labour and knew that despite the hours he'd spent repairing fences and fixing the doors on the barn, the Skivver home was no safer than it had been before he arrived. Nothing anyone could do would make the place impregnable to an attack by armed men. He began expressing his concern for the safety of Lottie and her parents but she interrupted him before he'd uttered many words.

'We aren't leaving,' she said, locking her eyes on his in an effort to forbid argument.

Nonetheless, Ben spoke his advice. 'You should get your father onto the wagon and go and stay with one of your neighbours.'

'Mr Petterfield wanted us to go back with him,' she confided, 'but Pa won't go. We'll have no home to return to if we leave it empty for a day. You know that as well as I do.'

'Let me talk to your father.'

'It won't do any good. He won't change his mind, and Ma and I won't let him stay alone.'

'Lottie! At the moment, your father isn't in any position to stand up for his principles.'

'You want him to run away?'

It seemed to Ben that the flash that showed in her

eyes was one of anger, as though she was holding back the additional words, 'like you.'

'Life is cheap to people like Col Brodie,' he told her, 'and the weaker their quarry, the easier the kill and the greater their enjoyment. I'm just suggesting that you band together. Individually, you're not a match for their strength. They'll pick you off one at a time.'

Lottie lowered her gaze and fixed her eyes on the ground at her feet. When she raised her head again some of the colour had left her face, marking her understanding of the severity of the threat faced by her family: that all of her family faced death if they remained in their home. A slight tremble of her lower lip betrayed a natural nervousness and the bright light of anger that Ben had observed only a moment earlier had been extinguished, lost behind a cloudiness that seemed to threaten rain. But it never came. Lottie pulled her shoulders back. 'My father won't surrender this land without a fight and my mother won't leave my father. I wasn't brought up to disrespect the decisions of my parents.'

For the moment, it was clear to Ben that further argument was pointless. 'I need to get Mrs Tippett back to town,' he said, and went into the barn to harness the livery horse to the buggy.

While he worked, Ben worried about the predicament of the settlers. As he'd told Lottie, unless they united and met the cattlemen's force head-on they were unlikely to survive. He had sympathy with their determination to hang onto their homes but he was honest enough to admit that in other circumstances he wouldn't even consider becoming involved. Lottie Skivver was the difference and he knew he couldn't desert her and leave her to the villainy of men like Col Brodie. If he was able to talk to Drew Skivver it was possible that he could persuade him to quit the farm, at least until he was more able to protect his family. Ben resolved to return to the Skivver farm before nightfall. Previous attacks on the homes of the settler families had always been carried out at night, at a time when the tired farmers were asleep in their beds and unable to mount any kind of resistance until fences had been pulled down, livestock scattered and vegetable gardens ridden through and destroyed. Ben had no reason to believe that any raid to press home the need for the weakened Drew Skivver to leave his home would be any different.

A brusque Gus Remarque had spoken to Col Brodie, Jarvis Wilson and Gatt Stone when they rode into the Long-R yard. He didn't even give them time to dismount.

'A man with a hole in his gun arm is no good to me,' he'd snapped at Gatt, who still carried his left arm in a sling.

'It's not my gun arm and I'll be rid of this sling in a day or two.'

'This business might be over in a day or two and I'm not using you or paying you until I'm sure you're capable of completing any task I give you. So you might as well go back to Pecos and stay there until you're useful to me.'

'If he goes then I go too,' Jarvis Wilson said.

'Fine, but no work no pay.'

'We've come a long way on a promise of two hundred dollars each,' Wilson said. 'You owe us that for what we've spent to get here and for rooms and meals in Pecos.'

'Cost of your rooms will be covered but only for three days unless you turn up here fit to do the work you've been hired for.'

'We'll be back,' Jarvis Wilson promised.

'Could be you won't be needed. Things are going so well that Brodie here might put an end to it today.'

Jarvis Wilson and Gatt Stone glowered at the rancher then turned their mounts and rode away.

The rancher had then turned his attention to the remaining hired gun. Col Brodie's face showed amusement at the exchange to which he'd been listening. He leant forward with his hands folded and pressed on the saddle-horn.

'You did well yesterday,' Gus Remarque said. 'I've got your bonus ready for collection whenever you want it, but first I want you to ride out to the Skivver place. My boys gave him a taste of the trouble that could come his way if he hangs about on that plot of land he's farming. He's the kingpin of the settler's resistance. No one will hang around if he's persuaded to leave.'

Brodie nodded slowly, assuring the rancher that he understood the situation.

'No need to be too heavy on this visit,' continued

Gus Remarque. 'He's probably unable to defend himself or his family, and a visit from the man who killed his neighbour might prove persuasive enough for him to load his wagon and get out of the territory. That's all that's needed this time; we can get rougher if it becomes necessary. If you get rid of him and the rest follow, you'll be richer by a thousand dollars.'

It was a generous sum for a job that had turned out to be easier than Brodie had anticipated.

'And if they've quit the territory without any need for me to use Wilson and Stone then you can have their bonus too. Another five hundred dollars.'

'Reckon I'll beat a trail north,' Brodie said. 'No time to lose.'

So he'd cut a trail that kept him on the east bank of the river, kept him clear of the town of Pecos and brought him to within four hundred yards of the farmhouse via a cleft between low-rising hummocks. He paused, watching the yard and buildings for movement but it wasn't until he began to move forward that he saw the motionless figure leaning against the yard rails. His immediate suspicion was that a guard had been posted. He eased the Colt in the holster tied to his right thigh, letting it slip back into position after assuring himself it would come clear of leather if that became a necessity.

It wasn't until he was halfway to the rails that he dismissed the idea that the person in the yard was a lookout. Although he was walking his horse so that its footfalls were almost silent on the grassy pasture, any vigilant person would still have seen him. He was twenty yards short of the gate when he realized that the slight figure beyond the rails was neither a man nor showing concern for anything beyond the confines of her railed compound. In fact, it was only a snuffling sound from his horse that drew her attention to him. She jumped back a step when she was aware of the rider's sudden closeness and, rather than being calmed by the action, her alarm grew when he pushed his hat up off his brow and grinned. 'Well, well,' he said, 'now I know why this stretch of land has such a high value.'

'Who are you?' Lottie wanted to know.

'Just open the gate and I'll introduce myself.'

Lottie didn't move. Strangers never travelled in this direction. Other settlers were the only people who called at their home. In addition, there was something unsettling about this man's manner.

'You must be Drew Skivver's daughter,' Brodie said. 'Reckon your pa will be expecting me.'

'Who are you?' Lottie asked again.

'I'm the man with the answer to all your family's troubles. You go and tell your pa that Col Brodie is here to see him.'

Lottie had never seen the man before but his name had bounced around their house when their neighbours had gathered the previous night. 'Go away,' she told him.

He laughed and leant forward to open the gate into the compound.

'Don't do that,' a voice ordered. Ben Joyner had finished tying the shafts of the buggy to the harness on the horse when the low voices had reached him, and it had taken only a glance to identify the horseman beyond the rail. In Pecos, Ben had been amused by Elsa Tippett's insistence on bringing with her the rifle that had belonged to Mr Raine, but now, as he stood outside the barn door, it was held purposely in his hands.

Col Brodie saw the rifle and lifted his hand from the gate. Then he looked at the man behind the gun. 'Mister, I don't like people who point guns at me.'

'Then take the young woman's advice and go away. You've got no business here.'

Slowly, Col Brodie straightened his back, his right hand now poised somewhere close to the butt of his pistol, threatening.

Ben Joyner moved his rifle slightly to make it clear to Brodie that the barrel was pointing at his belly. 'If you attempt to draw that gun, you'll have about the same chance of success as you gave the Dutchman yesterday. I don't think you're as brave as he was.'

Brodie stared at Ben Joyner. 'Tell Skivver that the beating he took yesterday will seem like a pat on the back compared to the landslide of trouble that's going to hit him and his neighbours if they don't leave this territory. You've got until tomorrow night. Then we'll see how brave you are.'

Brodie tugged at the reins, his horse stepped backwards and its head turned to the right as though about to turn away from the fence. Brodie kept his gaze fixed on Ben. 'I'll remember you,' he said. He turned his attention to Lottie. 'And you.' He raised his hand, removed his hat and executed an elaborate bow, sweeping his arm back at shoulder height and lowering his head until it almost touched his horse's neck. As he came upright he brought his arm forward and when it reached his waist he dropped his hat and pulled his gun from its holster. The manoeuvre had been enacted to throw Ben off-guard, to allow his own speed with a handgun to dominate their argument.

Ben's wartime experiences, however, had taught him never to relax until certain that the enemy was incapable of fight. He remained alert, ready for every ploy of his opponent. When he saw Brodie discard his hat to leave his hand free to grab for his weapon, Ben didn't hesitate. He pulled the trigger. The bullet ripped into Brodie's gut, as did the second one. Brodie squealed and slumped forward, hanging precariously around his horse's neck. The animal turned and Ben and Lottie could see the tatters and bloodstains around the points on the rider's back where the bullets had exited. Ben fire a third shot that passed close to the animal's tail, sending it galloping towards the low mounds from which it had emerged earlier.

SEVEN

Ben Joyner stood beside Lottie Skivver watching the running horse with its rider slumped forward on its neck. How far Col Brodie got before he fell off or was found was immaterial to Ben. He knew that Brodie would not survive the shooting and that he would suffer great agony before death claimed him. He wasn't troubled by that knowledge; Col Brodie would have dealt out the same to him if he'd been allowed to gain the upper hand.

Before the horse was out of sight, Drew Skivver had made his way awkwardly onto the porch of his small house. His wife and Elsa Tippett were with him, all three anxious to know the reason for the shooting. After listening to Ben's account, he expressed concern that Gus Remarque would seek retribution by launching an assault on his home.

Ben tried to quell his fears. 'Wherever the body is found there won't be any proof that Brodie ever came here, and even if it's suspected that he did, he'd only been sent to scare you, to give you a couple of days in which to pack up and leave the territory. The loss of his gunman won't please Mr Remarque, but he has other men to do his bidding so he has little need to change his plans. A raid tonight seems unlikely.'

It was Ben's hope that the Skivver family would use the respite to find refuge with the Petterfields or one of their other neighbours but the determination that was etched in his friend's face told him that that was not an option under consideration. Lottie, too, who had been quiet since the shooting, was as unwavering in support of her father's decision as she had been earlier. Her resolve to protect her home showed in the steady manner in which her pale blue eyes met his own. Given time and opportunity, he thought, he might be able to persuade Drew that, currently, he wasn't able to protect his family single-handed.

'I'll be back before nightfall,' he said, and when he received no argument, added, 'I'll keep watch in the barn overnight and hope to foil any raid by Long-R riders.'

Elsa Tippett nursed her rifle all the way back to Pecos, running her hands along the barrel as though the retained heat was a source of comfort. Most of the journey was conducted in silence. Even though Elsa had confirmed that the Skivvers had been acquainted with her kin, her mood had been little affected by the knowledge. She had learned that Henry and Lottie, being roughly the same age, had spent a lot of time together and that his oft-proclaimed pride in his home state had earned him the nickname the Ohio Kid, but if she'd gained any satisfaction in the knowledge that Pecos had, indeed, been the proposed destination of her men-folk, she was keeping it tight within. Ben could envisage possible enquiries she could make at hotels and stores, and conversations she could conduct with lawmen and tradesmen that might jog memories. They might progress her search for Henry and Carlton but, against that, the two-year void was probably a more definite indicator that they would never be traced.

'Is Mr Remarque the only cattleman opposed to the families that are settling in this area?' she asked Ben as they approached Pecos.

'All the cattlemen want to keep the grazing land for their herds.'

'But he's the only one trying to force them off their land.'

Ben figured that all the ranchers were in agreement with Gus Remarque's tactics but, for the moment, weren't prepared to dirty their hands with deeds of violence. They would happily reap the benefits of his success but, if things went wrong, they would have no awkward questions to answer if officers from Fort Worth came to investigate. That was a situation that wouldn't cause Gus Remarque to lose sleep. He saw himself as the prominent man in the area and not only was leading by example second nature to him, but he had grown pompous enough to regard the passivity of his neighbours as a show of respect, obeisance to his right to carry out his plans without interference.

Those thoughts were in Ben's mind but, when he failed to express them aloud instantly, Mrs Tippett spoke again. 'Is the Long-R the closest ranch to the settler families?'

'No. Mr Remarque's domain is south of Pecos, which is currently free of newcomers, but that's likely to alter if more people are attracted to this part of Texas. It's the cattlemen's opinion that there isn't a blade more grass here than is needed to feed their herds.'

Mrs Tippett didn't answer and didn't utter another word until they reached town.

After crossing the bridge, both Ben and Elsa Tippett became aware of the unusual atmosphere in which the main street seemed to be swathed. There seemed to be little humour shared among the people who had stopped to gossip along the sidewalks. Those men and women who bothered to turn their heads at the passing buggy all wore grim expressions, the recipients, perhaps, of unwelcome news. The focus of their attention was the congregation of men around a wagon further up the street. Ben estimated that it had come to a halt outside the sheriff's office, which they would have to pass on their way to the Alamo Hotel.

Across the street from the wagon a man was climbing onto a horse, and soon he had it running along the street towards the bridge. When he was level with the buggy he hauled his mount to a halt suddenly. Ben had recognized him moments earlier and had stopped his own vehicle in order to speak to the older man.

'Thought you had gone east,' Marty Levin said.

'Got caught up in a job bringing Mrs Tippett to Pecos.' Ben introduced Elsa Tippett to his former ranch companion.

Marty tipped his hat but his words were spoken to Ben. 'Got to get back to the Long-R,' he said. 'Mr Remarque will want to know that somebody killed Col Brodie.'

''That's the man who killed the Dutchman,' Ben said softly, feigning ignorance of the gunman's death and disassembling any suspicion of involvement that might have been triggered by his arrival in town so hot on the heels of the body.

'Yeah, well I suppose you had foresight of the way things would turn out.'

A spark of annoyance flashed in Ben. He didn't congratulate himself for being right; his prediction of the violence that had erupted on the streets of Pecos wasn't a cause for celebration. But Marty had sat up in the saddle, eager to put spurs to his horse. He cast another look at Elsa Tippett as though unwilling to say anything more while she was within earshot. 'We need to talk,' he told Ben, 'perhaps I'll see you later.'

'I'm busy tonight,' Ben told him. 'I'll find you tomorrow.'

Marty looked as though he was preparing an argument but, instead, gave a curt nod then rode away.

*

Ben Joyner ate a steak meal in a restaurant then saddled the chestnut and rode back to the Skivver homestead before darkness had fallen and the moon had risen. As he suspected, there was no attack on the house that night: crops and livestock remained untroubled. Hay in the loft provided warm and comfortable bedding for Ben and he took advantage of it when the position of the Big Dipper told him it was two hours gone midnight and too late for Long-R night-callers.

Before taking up his post in the barn, he had tried once more to persuade Drew Skivver to quit his home temporarily, recommending that he join forces with one of his neighbours. However, even stressing the need to protect his women-folk didn't prove argument enough to sway Drew from his determination to stay on the patch of land he called his own.

'I appreciate you coming out here tonight,' Drew told Ben. 'It puts you in opposition to men you've ridden beside.'

Ben hadn't ridden with men like Col Brodie and had no wish to share a bunkhouse with men who were prepared to emulate the brutal behaviour of that gunslinger. Despite his action earlier in the day, Ben was reluctant to use guns. When facing Col Brodie, however, there had been no alternative. 'I'll come out while you need me,' he said. His major worry was that Gus Remarque's men would come raiding when he wasn't here. His second worry was that he would be ineffectual against a determined attack if he were here.

He was halfway between the house and barn when Lottie followed him outside with a blanket folded over her arm. The night hadn't yet lost all of the heat of the day and the neck-high, blue wool dress she wore ensured that she wasn't chilled by the slight breeze that came from across the river. Yet Ben detected a tiny tremble as she passed the blanket to him. Her eyes were big when she looked into his face, and it seemed that there were questions she wanted to ask that hung unspoken on her lips.

'Are you cold?' asked Ben.

She shook her head.

He wondered if she was affected by the tension of the situation, a reaction perhaps to the shooting she'd witnessed earlier and the possibility of an attack on her home by violent men. Ben tried to reassure her. 'I don't expect there'll be any trouble tonight.'

'Why are you here?' she asked, the question almost blurted out, eager for an answer as though it held the key to her future. But the words ended abruptly, conveying regret that they had been released into the night, almost fearing the answer she might receive.

'I was obliged to bring Mrs Tippett through the brush country,' Ben told her, the intonation expressing surprise; he'd explained earlier the events that had brought him back to Pecos.

A glint of moonlight flashed in Lottie's eyes. 'I meant here, tonight. Why have you come back to our home?' She knew it was a question she shouldn't ask, shouldn't try to trap him into giving an answer that would commit him to a decision that he might not make freely. More worryingly, it might persuade him to ride away in the morning and never return.

'I don't mean to belittle your pa, Lottie, but with a busted arm he isn't able to put up much resistance against a bunch of raiders.'

'You've made it clear it's not your fight,' she said.

'I think the events earlier in the day altered that. Can't let you and your family be called to account for my actions.'

Ben had spoken the truth: he fought his own fights and this one had become his the moment Col Brodie had ridden up to threaten Drew Skivver and his family. Ben admired Drew Skivver and wasn't prepared to stand aside while his home and everything he'd worked for was destroyed. Of course, the safety of Lottie Skivver had figured large in the cause of Ben's intervention. Two weeks earlier he'd quit Pecos when there had been little more than a suggestion that Gus Remarque's antagonism would escalate into violence. It was possible that the Skivvers and everyone else who had staked out land along the river might have prospered without any conflict developing with the cattlemen. Now it was different. Blood had been spilt and more would soak the ground before the matter was settled. When the killing began it was difficult to stop, and if the boss of the Long-R wanted retribution for the slaying of his hired gun then he would find Ben Joyner ready for combat.

Although he'd left Pecos once, and it was clear that Lottie suspected he would do so again, Ben knew he couldn't go while she was in jeopardy. He couldn't go until her father was once again able to bear arms. Perhaps not even then.

Lottie raised her head, a gesture like her father's when he had a point to make. 'You don't need to feel compelled to fight on our behalf. Mr Remarque is not going to run us off land we rightly own. If you go away again, we'll understand.'

'Is that what you want, Lottie? Do you want me to ride away and forget you?'

Lottie opened her mouth. Words were waiting to spill out, a declaration that she doubted that her wishes had any influence over his decisions, but they were never uttered. Her head drooped slightly so that she was no longer looking into his eyes.

'I mean to stay here and help,' Ben said, 'and I won't leave until you tell me to go.'

EIGHT

Next morning, while Ben Joyner shared breakfast with the Skivver family, Jarvis Wilson and Gatt Stone were meeting with Gus Remarque, who had summoned them to the Lazy-R. Gatt's left arm was no longer in a sling; he wanted the money he'd been promised and was prepared to suffer the ache in his shoulder to convince the rancher that he was capable of earning it.

Gus Remarque noted how Gatt favoured his left arm as he climbed down from his saddle but didn't comment. Col Brodie's death had, for the moment, left him with little choice other than to use these two men to complete the job of hassling the settlers away from the northern grassland. His foreman, Davey Pursur, had hinted that the recent increase of violence might have weakened any lingering thoughts of resistance among the settlers and that already they might be preparing to leave the territory. If that were so, then recruiting more people to enforce his views would serve no purpose. By the time they got here there might be no problem to solve.

'What news from Pecos?' the rancher wanted to know. 'Who was celebrating Brodie's death last night?'

'Nobody, Mr Remarque,' Jarvis Wilson replied.

The rancher was doubtful that that was the truth of the matter. 'No one bragging that they were responsible for clipping him? No glasses raised among the settler people?'

'None of them came to town last night. If they were celebrating they were doing it in their own homes.'

'None!' Gus Remarque assessed that information, muttering the thoughts that arose from his musing. 'Either they've figured out some scheme to keep clear of Pecos in the hope of avoiding trouble or they've had enough and are busy packing their belongings.' He looked at the two men who stood before him, judging their competence before assigning a task. 'I assume you are capable of riding and using your eyes.' His stare was fixed on Gatt Stone, leaving that man in no doubt that he wasn't fooled by the discarded arm-sling. 'Well, I don't suppose you can get into trouble just watching the activities of the settlers,' he said.

'What do you want us to do?' asked Jarvis Wilson.

'Find out what the settlers are doing. If they're sensible they'll be loading their wagons, but I need to know for sure. Visit every homestead but don't get embroiled with the people. Observe, then report back here tonight.'

'You want us to spend time in Pecos, too, pick up the gossip on who killed Brodie?'

'No need,' Gus Remarque told him, 'I'll go and speak to Sheriff Vasey myself.'

Gus Remarque watched the gunmen ride away then ordered Davey Pursur to saddle his horse. 'I'm going into Pecos.'

'Do you want me to come with you?'

'Yes, and another man. Whoever was lucky enough to get the better of Col Brodie might have garnered the confidence to make a play against me.'

The frustration generated by his injuries was a greater source of annoyance to Drew Skivver than the pain they occasioned, and more difficult to hide. Inactivity was a stranger to him and one that would never become his boon companion. Even breakfast had been a trial to him, and the fussing by his wife and daughter had blunted his appetite rather than encouraged him to eat it.

'I can't do anything,' he grumbled to Ben Joyner as the latter threw his saddle over the chestnut.

'Face it, Drew: it'll take a few weeks before you can use both hands again, but don't let it defeat you. I've seen ranch hands overcome unbelievable injuries and adapt their working practices to take on tasks they didn't think possible. Over time, you'll do it, too.'

'That's the problem,' his friend said, 'I'm not blessed with patience and I can't leave all the work to Sarah and Lottie. I'm already asking too much of them, risking their lives by staying here when so much danger threatens. I talk big, Ben, but I know I can't protect my family the way I ought to. I suspect you're right: I should abandon this place and move in with Jonas until this matter is settled.'

Ben Joyner almost permitted himself a grin. Overnight, they had both reversed their thinking. His family's safety had forced Drew to reconsider the firm stand he'd made to hang on to his home while, at the same time, Ben had been convinced by Lottie's impassioned loyalty to her father that any weakness shown would surely lead to the loss of the land that was legally theirs.

'I told Lottie I would stay to help as long as you need me,' he said.

'Lottie,' repeated Drew. Something in the way Ben had spoken his daughter's name informed him that there was greater meaning behind the young man's words. 'Well, that's good. That's good.'

Ben led the chestnut outside and climbed into the saddle. 'I'll be back before nightfall,' he said. He saw Lottie near the house and touched the brim of his hat. She didn't answer with any extravagant gesture but her facial muscles which, the previous day, had been tight with concern, were now eased and her eyes were open wider to flash their blueness at him. Words weren't necessary. An understanding existed that would be voiced when the trouble that currently hung over them had been resolved.

At first, Ben followed the river, but veered from the trail when he was yet two miles from the bridge that crossed into Pecos. He rode at a steady pace, allowing the chestnut to eat up the ground as he made his way towards the pastures that were used by the Long-R herds. The look he'd seen in Marty Levin's eyes when they'd met in Pecos had held a message and a need to deliver it urgently. So Ben had determined to seek out his old friend by riding those sections of the range where cattle were most likely grazing.

It had only been two weeks since he'd been a member of the Long-R crew so had no reason to believe that any herders he came across would be hostile towards him, yet the situation had changed while he'd been away, and if it was known that he'd spent time at the home of the Skivver family then his loyalty to the cattlemen's cause would surely be questioned. Accordingly, those working groups he encountered during the morning he observed from a distance, and when he was sure that Marty Levin was not among the riders he rode on without approaching the others.

He was several miles south of Pecos, nearing the Long-R ranch itself, when he had the first inkling that perhaps he was under observation from someone riding the ridge to his right. Stones had rolled and, when he'd looked up, unidentifiable shadows had flitted across the ground but there had been no substantial evidence to back-up his unease. Unsure if his suspicion was merely a trick of the mind, he'd ridden on. He was travelling at walking pace, his eyes at one moment fixed on the ridge to his right then, at the next, sweeping the flat terrain to his left that led to the Long-R ranch house.

It was riders coming across the grassland that he spotted first, two quick-moving, distant and unidentifiable dots. Ben reined to a halt to watch their approach, wondering once more what reception he might receive from men with whom he'd recently shared a bunkhouse, grub and duties. But at that moment, a movement to his right caught his attention, a flash as sunlight reflected off bright metal and, although he couldn't see him, Ben knew that a horseman had stopped on the ridge above. Reacting instantly, he turned the chestnut and retraced his own tracks for a dozen yards to seek out a path that climbed the short, steep hillside. Instinct told him that discovering the identity of the person who had stalked him for almost a mile was more important than an encounter with former ranch-hands.

Winding through the trees, he reached the rim of the high ground at a point behind the place he expected to find the rider. A horse, reins trailing the ground, stood peacefully thirty yards away. Its saddle was empty. Ben dismounted and moved forward cautiously. Carefully, avoiding putting his feet down where they might disturb stones or crack twigs, he advanced towards the horse, letting his gaze wander in search of its owner. At the edge of the rim a figure was using the trunk of a willow that leant out from the hillside, thereby providing an unobstructed view across the grasslands below. Whoever it was, if they were trying to catch a glimpse of him, they were looking in the wrong direction.

There was something familiar about the flat-crowned hat that had been pushed up from the brow to sit on the back of the head. Ben noted the neatness of shirt and trousers, too clean for a cattle-herder, which dismissed the notion that his tracker was a curious member of one of the groups he'd passed earlier. It was only when the watcher moved, shifted and began to walk around the tree that he realized that the person under his gaze was a woman.

'Are you looking for me, Mrs Tippett?' he asked.

Startled, Elsa Tippett swung around to face him. 'No.'

'You were following me.'

Elsa Tippett denied it.

'You've been riding the ridge, keeping pace with me.'

'I was not following you,' she insisted.

'What are you doing here?'

'Getting to know the territory. Is that so strange?'

'South of Pecos you're likely to stray on to Mr Remarque's land. He doesn't welcome trespassers at any time and it could be dangerous to fall foul of him while a war is brewing with the settlers.'

'Are you saying he would do me harm?'

Ben wasn't sure what Gus Remarque would do. He had little reason, however, to believe that punishment meted out to those he considered a threat would be mitigated by sex. He hired gunfighters to achieve his ambitions. He was ruthless.

'I mean to have a look around,' Elsa Tippett continued. 'Mr Skivver told me that my son had earmarked a section of land in this vicinity. I want to see it.'

Ben shook his head, exasperated. 'Go back to Pecos, Mrs Tippett,' he said. He figured his words were a waste of breath; the woman hadn't complied with anything he'd said in the past and it was unlikely she would do so in the future, even though he was trying to be helpful.

She didn't answer. Instead, the look in her eyes hardened but Ben didn't believe her change of demeanour was caused by his instruction. Her gaze was focused on something beyond his left shoulder, and the rattle of bridle fixings prompted him to turn around to investigate. Ben guessed that the two men who were now before him were the pair he had seen crossing the grasslands when he'd begun the climb up to the ridge. Also, they were the pair he had hoped to avoid during his stay in Pecos.

Jarvis Wilson was still astride his horse, his hands placed one atop the other on the saddle horn. The glint in his eyes was as cold as ice but his lips twitched as though having difficulty suppressing a smile.

Gatt Stone was on his feet, the reins of his own horse and those of Ben's chestnut gripped in his left hand while a cocked pistol was held awkwardly in the other. There was no play in the expression on his face: revenge was his spur and murder his intent. 'You were right, Jarv,' he muttered, 'you said we'd soon run into him again.'

Jarvis Wilson's reply was to cease the struggle with his facial muscles and a smile spread across his face.

'Revenge for me and a new horse for you, isn't that what you said?'

'My very words.'

Gatt gestured with his pistol for Ben to unbuckle his gun belt.

'This doesn't concern Mrs Tippett,' Ben said as his holstered weapon fell to the ground. He knew there was little he could to protect the woman but his natural instinct was to seek out every small advantage he could provide for her. At that moment it seemed that nothing he could do would be adequate to save her from the guns of the men they faced, but by manoeuvring his body he pushed closer to the tree, hoping its gnarled, old trunk might protect her when the shooting began.

'Of course it doesn't.' Jarvis Wilson twisted in the saddle and studied the unattended horse that peacefully grazed a few yards away. 'That must be your mount, Mrs Tippett. It carried you here so I reckon it's able to carry you back to Pecos.' He swept his arm in a gesture that inferred she was free to climb into the saddle and ride away.

Elsa Tippet didn't move. Ben knew she had fixed her gaze on him. For once, he thought, she was prepared to listen to his advice but none came immediately to his mind. Despite what he said, Ben didn't believe that Jarvis Wilson was prepared to let Elsa Tippett ride away. They intended to kill him and couldn't allow any witnesses to survive.

'I'll go when Mr Joyner goes,' Elsa Tippett announced.

'Mr Joyner and I have matters to discuss. He could be here for some time.'

'Even so,' Elsa Tippett spoke defiantly, making it clear that she was aware of the nature of things and was gambling that her presence would avoid bloodshed.

The supercilious grin that had developed during the brief exchange remained intact on the face of Jarvis Wilson. 'That makes things so much easier for me,' he said and, with a sudden movement, drew his pistol from its holster and fired a shot. The bullet struck the ground behind the legs of Mrs Tippett's horse, sending it off on a startled run along the ridge.

Those few seconds that Jarvis Wilson had spent twisted in the saddle in order to stampede Elsa Tippett's horse proved vital to Ben Joyner. Not only had the rider taken his eyes off the pair he intended to kill, but his companion, too, had turned to watch the fleeing animal. Ben's reaction was instantaneous, moving even while the thought that another opportunity would never come his way channelled through his mind. Using his left arm, he pushed Elsa Tippett behind the tree; her surprised yelp and the knowledge that she was sprawled on the ground registered in his subconscious as he dipped his head and drove his body into the bulky form of Gatt Stone. Together they tumbled into the horses, the beasts backing away, feet stamping, heads thrown high and emitting a series of nervous sounds.

A gunshot cracked. Ben knew Gatt Stone hadn't

fired it because that man had almost lost the grip on his weapon when they landed in a heap on the ground. Ben knew he should be concerned about the safety of Elsa Tippett but for the moment the top priority was to wrestle the gun away from his opponent. They were under the legs of the horses now where, despite the risk of being struck by a flying hoof, Ben was afforded a degree of safety. Jarvis Wilson couldn't shoot at him without risk of wounding either the horse he desired or his companion.

Gatt was a man of brute strength who recovered quickly from the surprise attack. Immediately, he was using forearms, elbows and head in the manner of a man accustomed to street and barroom brawls. His intention was to shake off the grip that Ben had fastened around the wrist of the hand that held the gun but was having little success, hindered mainly by the shoulder that was still recovering from the impact of the slug that Ben had put into it several days ago. He twisted, turning rapidly in order to be uppermost. Both bodies bumped against the legs of the animals above, causing them to dance away, stepping gingerly across the men whose struggle was unabated by the risk of a blow from an iron-shod hoof.

Eventually, it was Gatt who suffered a blow from a fore hoof of Ben's chestnut. Anxious to move away from the underfoot obstacles, it had skipped backwards with its front legs raised and would have escaped the melee if, at that moment, Ben hadn't taken the opportunity to thrust his head into the other's face powerfully enough to inflict a cut above

Gatt's left eye from which blood began to run freely. Stunned, Gatt instinctively drew away from Ben, unmindful of the startled horses. The chestnut's hoof impacted with the already wounded shoulder, extracting a yell from Gatt that laid bare the agony that had been invoked.

The horses parted and Ben saw that his opponent had dropped the gun he'd been clinging to so grimly. Now it lay on the ground only inches from his own hand and possession of it could extract him and Elsa Tippett from the situation in which they found themselves. The solution, however, was not simple to achieve. The horses were no longer a barrier between himself and Jarvis Wilson; using Gatt as a buffer was currently the only impediment to being a clear target for the mounted man. The cold expression he saw on the other's face made it clear that waiting for the opportunity to kill him was merely adding to Jarvis Wilson's enjoyment of the situation.

'Try for it,' scoffed Wilson. 'I only want the horse. It's Gatt who wants to kill you.'

Ben didn't move. He was aware that Gatt's moans were lessening and that at any moment his hatred would overcome his pain and he would use the gun to fulfil the revenge that burned inside him.

'Now Mrs Tippett over there,' Wilson waggled the gun he held in the direction of the tree, 'offered me fifty dollars a few days ago. Payment is due now.' Almost casually, as though he had implicit faith in his marksmanship, he fired his pistol. A lump flew off the tree behind which Elsa Tippett waited. 'Come out, Mrs Tippett.'

'What's all the shooting about?' The voice was gruff and authoritative and it came from behind Jarvis Wilson.

Accompanied by Davey Pursur and Marty Levin, Gus Remaque made the final climb up to the summit of the ridge and regarded the tableau before him. His eyes settled first on Gatt Stone and a glint of disapproval showed in his eyes as he noted the way that man held his shoulder. It was apparent that the pain he was experiencing made him incapable of carrying out the work that was expected of him. The rancher's gaze flicked over Ben, registering surprise and curiosity when he recognized his former employee. It was only when he reined to a halt beside Jarvis Wilson that he spoke. 'Put that gun away,' he said.

It took a moment for Wilson to obey; the deliberate slowness with which he re-housed his weapon was meant to demonstrate both his reluctance to obey to Gus Remarque and a threat to Ben Joyner that it would be drawn again when next they met.

'So what is it all about?' Gus Remarque asked again.

By now, Davey Pursur and Marty Levin had drawn alongside their boss.

'Not for the first time, these men are trying to steal my horse,' Ben announced.

'These men are in my employment,' replied Gus Remarque. 'I'll need proof of that before I'll take any action against them.'

Ben knew that Gus Remarque wouldn't take action against men who were part of his own crew unless their crimes were against him personally. Nonetheless, he pointed at the chestnut that was watching from a point a dozen yards along the ridge. 'Do you recognize the horse, Mr Remarque?'

'I recognize the brand burned on its hip. That's the Long-R. My brand, which means the horse belongs to me.'

'The horse is mine. You sold him to me.'

Marty Levin shuffled in his saddle as though he had something to add to the conversation, but any support he had intended to give to Ben's case remained unspoken.

'Put a rope on it,' the rancher told his foreman. 'We'll sort out the matter another day.'

'The matter is sorted,' Ben told him. 'You know that horse belongs to me. Besides, I've got a bill of sale in my pocket, which has your signature on it. Do you mean to deny your own name? If you take that horse away I'll make it known all around Pecos that you've reneged on a bill of sale. There are plenty of people in that town who know the horse is mine, which will leave you with a reputation no better than that of a common horse thief. Who will trust or do business with you then?'

Angrily, Gus Remarque scowled. He was the self-styled king of the section and wielded the power to prove it. Saddle tramps had no right to speak to him in those terms. He examined the faces around him. 'Perhaps you shouldn't be so bold,' he said to Ben.

'All of these men take my dollar. They do my bidding. If I order it you'll be buried in these hills.'

Elsa Tippet, who had until this moment remained hidden behind the old willow, stepped forward. 'Do you also kill women?' she asked.

'Who are you?'

'My name is Elsa Tippett.'

'What are you doing here?'

'Trying to find my son and brother, Henry Tippett and Carlton Wellwin. Did you ever meet them?'

For a long moment, Gus Remarque stared at her. 'No,' he said then turned his attention to Wilson and Stone. 'When I give you two a job to do I don't expect you to put it aside to pursue your own petty grievances. Get mounted and attend to what you're being paid to do.'

The two men clambered into their saddles, one with a grin for Ben that was in no way friendly, and the other, less athletically, with a look like thunder, redolent of a man still seeking revenge but unsure that it would ever be achieved.

As Wilson and Stone rode away, Gus Remarque spoke again to Ben Joyner. 'You've got your horse. I suggest you use it to get out of this territory. If I see you on my land again I won't do anything to stop my men killing you.'

'This isn't your land, Mr Remarque: it's free range. You might use it to graze your cattle but you don't own it. Someday, perhaps someday soon, someone will own it, but until that time I'll ride in these hills as much as I choose.'

'I don't know why you're pushing me, boy, but after today don't cross me again, or I'll kill you myself.'

NINE

When he looked up, John Vasey was surprised to find that his paperwork was being interrupted by Gus Remarque. John had represented the law in Pecos for almost a decade and, to the best of his recollection, this was the first occasion that the region's most prominent man had entered his office. They weren't strangers, of course, but their conversations had rarely been more than a few words exchanged on the street or in one of the many saloons that adorned Austin Street. When the rancher wanted detailed information, he summoned the sheriff to the Long-R. There had been only two occasions when John had ridden out to the ranch uninvited: seeking the rancher's explanation for incidents it had become necessary to investigate.

John Vasey put aside his pen and waited for Gus Remarque to speak. Even if the older man had been a regular visitor in the past, the frown lines on his brow and the fact that he was accompanied by his foreman and Marty Levin made it clear that this day it was the rancher who was seeking information.

'What's going on in this town?' asked Gus, his voice accusatory, as though John Vasey was responsible for every evil act in Texas.

'Are you referring to anything in particular?' the sheriff replied, immediately irritated by the other's attitude. Gus Remarque's position in this area had never been in doubt and, until now, John Vasey had never had any reason to oppose it. However, he hadn't been able to dislodge from his mind the barb that Ben Joyner had slung at him the previous day – whose law did he uphold: that of Texas or Gus Remarque?

'A man was killed yesterday. Have you caught his killer yet?'

'If you mean Col Brodie, he was neither killed in this town nor was he a citizen of Pecos. His death isn't my concern.'

'Well, it's my concern. That man was working for me. Where was his body found?'

'Across the river. A teamster bringing in supplies from Amarillo found him about five miles out of town.'

'Bushwhacked by one of those settlers. You need to find out which one and hang him for murder.'

'You might have employed Col Brodie, Mr Remarque, but you don't employ me. The people of Pecos pay me to keep law and order in this town, not to go chasing wild geese across the rangeland. They might be more concerned by the fact that I didn't lock up your foreman and his pals for their cowardly and unprovoked attack on Drew Skivver.'

Davey Pursur stiffened, affronted by the sheriff's remark. 'Drew Skinner's a land thief,' he snarled.

'They are all land thieves,' said Gus Remarque, 'and they need to be cleared out of this area, pronto.'

'They have papers that give them a right to the land they've built their homes on.' Uttering those words was almost as much of a surprise to John Vasey himself as it was to the boss of the Long-R. Personally, he'd never had any problem with the influx of newcomers but because this was cow country he was aware that the needs of the stock were a rancher's paramount concern. Historically, the ranchers governed the territory and he'd supported them, but now his role was not so clear.

'Are you siding with the settlers?' Gus Remarque's words sounded as angry as the glare he directed at the sheriff.

'I'm siding with Pecos,' retorted John Vasey. 'The merchants in town welcome the business that the newcomers bring with them. They don't want them driven away.'

'The merchants survived well enough before they came. I reckon they will after they're gone.'

'*If* they go,' said the sheriff, 'and getting rid of them might not be as easy as you think.'

'What do you mean by that?'

'There's talk around town about sending for the Rangers. People don't want the place torn up with gunfights and battles. Think on it, Mr Remarque, and try to settle your differences with the newcomers because the Rangers are sure to support any papers issued by the state of Texas.'

For a moment, Gus Remarque was dumbstruck. The Texas Rangers were, indeed, a greater threat to him than a town officer with a star on his chest. He could cajole and manipulate men like John Vasey as easily as he could rope the hind legs of a yearling but the Rangers wielded the authority of the state. He could neither threaten nor hope to bamboozle them. Yet, despite the disquiet that had been aroused by that disclosure, Gus was more greatly troubled by the fact that it marked another instance of rebellion to the power he'd commanded in this region for twenty years. When he'd spoken, others had jumped to obey his commands. Now, in the space of a few days, he had been confronted by his foreman, threatened by a former employee and let down by men he'd hired for their specialist skills. Furthermore, the people he'd expected to be driven off the grassland were showing an unexpected determination to resist his plans, were preparing to fight, and victory for them would not only be humiliating but disastrous to his own affluence.

He turned away, reluctant to let the lawman see the perturbation that undoubtedly showed on his face, and as he did so his eyes lit on two riders who were passing along the street at that time. Ben Joyner and Elsa Tippett had arrived back in Pecos quicker than he'd expected and were now riding along Austin Street with a boldness that told the rancher that they had no intention of heeding his instruction to get out of town. Regret seeped through him. If, earlier, he'd allowed Wilson and the useless Stone to proceed unhindered then the pair now dismounting outside the Alamo Hotel would no longer be a potential source of trouble. Joyner had spoken to him like a man with a grievance, as though they had always been enemies, but it was the woman who troubled him most.

'Tippett,' he murmured, then, aloud, spoke to John Vasey. 'I want those two out of town before another twenty-four hours have passed.'

The sheriff was on the point of arguing but Gus Remarque didn't give him the opportunity. He opened the door and stepped out onto the street with his foreman and Marty Levin at his heels. As they walked away from the sheriff's office, Gus spoke first to Marty Levin.

'Ride out to the northern ranches,' he told the cowboy. 'Tell Carter, Wainwright and Johnson to be here in Pecos for ten o'clock tomorrow. No excuses. If the settlers want a fight then we'll give them one.'

Marty Levin clambered into his saddle and headed back towards the bridge over the Pecos River.

'Davey,' Gus said after Marty's departure, 'I'm staying in town tonight. I want you to go back to the ranch and organise tomorrow's work, but I want you back here before ten. Bring some men with you ready to fight.'

'Sure thing, boss,' came the reply, and he, too, rode out of Pecos while Gus Remarque crossed the street to the Alamo where a room was always available to him.

Among the old adobe buildings that constituted the Mexican old town was the single-storied cantina owned by Pedro Garcia. The only natural light that penetrated the low-ceilinged interior came via the ever open door, lighting up little more than a rectangle of floor which altered in size and location in accordance with the position of the shifting sun. Those who weren't regular customers, especially those Americans who had been attracted by the spicy smells that wafted from within, always chose a table as close as possible to the patch of daylight, as though compelled to inspect the food that was presented to them by Pedro or his wife. Although Marty Levin was no stranger to the *cantina* he still put his hat on the first table and sat facing the door so that the sunlight fell on his plate of fried beans, chicken and sweet potatoes. His reason for choosing that location, however, had nothing to do with distrust of the fare put before him but a need to keep an eye open for discovery by Davey Pursur. Gus Remarque had given him a direct order and would expect it to be obeyed without delay but Marty was hungry and if he were to deliver a message to all the northern ranchers he wouldn't get back to the Long-R until the cook had stacked away his pans. So he'd ridden away from Austin Street but had dismounted at Pedro Garcia's *cantina* before crossing the river.

Marty was lifting the first forkful of food to his

mouth when he saw Davey Pursur leave town. When the foreman passed by without casting a glance in the direction of the *cantina*, Marty was able to relax and enjoy the meal. Shortly after, however, another rider caught his eye, this one, too, heading for the bridge across the Pecos. Hurriedly, Marty forked more food into his mouth, dropped some coins onto the table then rushed outside. He'd hitched his horse to a rail behind the cantina so that it wouldn't attract the attention of anyone from the Long-R but he was soon in the saddle and riding clear of the town.

The second rider had been Ben Joyner and, following the earlier confrontation with Gus Remarque, Marty deemed it unlikely that he was once more heading for the territory around the Long-R. He guessed that, like himself, Ben's business was taking him north but their destinations were the homes of opposing forces. Marty's horse covered the ground at a steady, loping run and he came within sight of Ben about two miles outside town.

Following the events of the morning, Ben's initial instinct was to place his hand on the butt of his pistol when he heard the sound of a rapidly approaching rider. He watched the horseman for several seconds before recognizing the riding style and eventually the features of his former Long-R companion. Ben halted his horse and waited for the older man to reach him.

Marty's first words contained no hint of a greeting, delivered in a growling tone that reflected the scowl on his face and signified an anger within. 'Thought you'd left the territory,' he said. 'Gone to build a railway or find gold or push beef someplace where the grass is better than Pecos scrubland.'

'I went. I came back.'

'You should have stayed away. You didn't want to fight when you were employed by Mr Remarque but you seem eager now to pitch in against him.'

'Back then, I had no interest in the fate of either Mr Remarque's cattle or the homes of the settlers, but that's changed.'

Marty pushed his hat to the back of his head. 'The Skivver girl,' he said, his voice still gruff, but its crustiness merely covering his understanding and an acknowledgement that the suspicions he'd voiced weeks earlier were now confirmed. 'The settlers can't win a fight against the cattlemen. If you want to help them then advise them to take up Mr Remarque's offer for their land. No need for anyone to get killed if they quit the land.'

'People have been killed already,' Ben said, 'but no need for anymore if the families are allowed to work their land in peace.'

'The cattlemen need the grass,' Marty said, knowing that those words hadn't the power to sway his friend from the views he held.

'And killers have been brought in to take it, to steal what is not legally theirs.'

'Wilson and Stone,' Marty said, naming the duo he supposed were uppermost in Ben's mind. 'I overheard them talking about you, discussing what they would do to you when they caught you. They found you this morning before I was able to warn you.'

'That wasn't their first attempt at my life.'

'How did you get involved with them?'

'They tried to steal my horse and I suspect I foiled their scheme to rob Mrs Tippett.'

'Tippett,' muttered Marty. 'Where did you meet her?'

'She was stranded in a small town across the scrubland. She'd come all the way from Ohio but her guide met with an accident and she needed someone to bring her on to Pecos.'

'Tippett,' Marty repeated, his eyes fixed on Ben. 'What business has she in Pecos?'

'Looking for her son and brother. Should have been among the families that settled hereabouts but they went missing after leaving Fort Worth. Everyone agrees that this was their destination.'

Marty was unmoving, as still as a wooden Indian outside a small town emporium. 'Who was her guide?' he asked.

'A man called Raine. Brad Raine. I guess it's the same man who once worked at the Long-R.'

Marty nodded. 'Same man,' he agreed.

'He convinced Mrs Tippett that her men-folk came to Pecos so perhaps he met them. Did you come across them, Marty?'

Marty Levin didn't answer the question. Instead, he said, 'That woman is trouble.'

'Trouble for who, Marty?'

'You, if you persist in helping her.'

'What do you know, Marty? Did you meet Henry

Tippett and Carlton Wellwin?'

'I know they're dead and nothing anybody does or says will change that. So pack up your roll, Ben, and get out of Pecos.'

'You know they're dead?' Ben repeated, but it was the other man's querulous manner rather than his words that had the greater affect on him. 'What do you know about their deaths, what happened?'

'There's nothing more to say. Forget about it, Ben.'

Ben didn't agree with the Long-R rider. There was a lot more to say. 'A woman has travelled across the continent to find out what happened to her son and brother. She deserves to know what happened.'

'They were rustlers,' blurted Marty.

Ben Joyner almost smiled. All he'd heard about young Henry Tippett and his uncle had portrayed them as carefree ex-soldiers eager to find a place to settle down and work the land. No one had hinted that they were likely to operate outside the law. But as the accusation settled in his mind, so did the consequences that befell those who were caught with another man's cattle. 'You hanged them,' he said. Even as the words left his mouth he recalled sitting alongside Marty under a tree from which two men had been hanged, and Marty telling him about the slaughter of Mexican shepherds and their flock but dismissive of the lynching of rustlers.

'Did you catch them with the cattle?' he asked.

'What does it matter? What else would they be doing on Long-R ranch land?'

Ben wondered if they had been on Long-R ranch land or open range, but he didn't dwell on the matter. 'Passing through,' he suggested, then asked what reason they'd given.

Marty removed his hat and swatted it against his chest as though trying to beat out dust. He turned his head and cast looks right and left to scrutinise the empty space around them.

'What did they say?' urged Ben. 'I assume they were given the opportunity to defend themselves.'

'They said they'd bought that stretch of land.'

'Did they have a paper to prove it?'

'Mr Remarque said that nobody was stealing anything from him. Neither stock nor grazing land.'

'So you *lynched* them?'

'That's the way law is maintained,' snapped Marty.

'Remarque's law,' answered Ben.

'Cattlemen's law.'

'The same cattlemen's law used against the Mexican shepherds,' Ben reminded Marty. 'You know Gus Remarque was wrong then, and he was wrong to hang Henry Tippett and Carlton Wellwin.' A thought occurred to him. 'Was Brad Raine involved?'

Marty nodded. 'He spoke up for the rustlers. Mr Remarque threw him off the ranch next day. Shortly after that, settlers began to arrive, building their little farms along this part of the river.' He reset his hat and prepared to ride away. 'Whatever happened in the past doesn't alter the fact that Mr Remarque wants to reclaim the grazing land from the farmers.

I've got messages to deliver. My advice to you is to get out of the area immediately.'

Ben watched his former companion ride away. Thoughts of leaving weren't in his head. Uppermost in his mind was Elsa Tippett and the probabilities that she knew her kinsfolk were dead. It was learning that he, Ben, had not arrived at the Long-R until after Brad Raine quit the place that had lessened the tension of their journey across the scrubland. Had she insisted on travelling with him because she suspected he'd been one of the crew who had lynched her son, what would she have done if he had been?

TEN

In the presence of Gus Remarque, Gatt Stone had sat upright in the saddle, hiding his suffering. Already, the rancher was reluctant to keep him on the payroll and would surely renege on his promised payment if he surmised that the scuffle with Ben Joyner had resulted in him being less able to complete his job. It was the blow from the flailing horse hoof that had done the damage, striking him almost on the very spot where the bullet had punctured his flesh. But he'd kept a stoic expression and had tried to ignore the pain until he and Jarvis Wilson had ridden off to attend to the business that had sent them from the Long-R earlier that morning. Now, however, his body slumped in the saddle, his head drooped closer to his horse's neck. Excruciating spasms engulfed his shoulder with every jarring stride. He moaned and cursed as he tried to keep pace with his companion, and his brow was wet with feverish sweat.

Although Gatt's initial injury, the bullet he'd taken in the shoulder, had been acquired in pursuit of

Wilson's desire for Ben Joyner's chestnut, his companion offered no compassion. Indeed, the failure, once more, to gain possession of the chestnut had soured Jarvis Wilson's mood and the other man's continuous grumbling was as troublesome to him as a stone in his boot. He didn't look back once, although they rode for ten miles before stopping.

Beneath the grime and sweat, Gatt Stone's face was ashen as he stumbled from the saddle. Gratefully, he leant against a tree, bracing his body against the waves of pain that washed over him. 'Couldn't have gone much further,' he said.

Jarvis Wilson offered no comment but he was thinking that they couldn't go much further together. He wasn't prepared to share his money if Gus Remarque refused to pay Gatt, and that seemed more probable every day. The sooner word was given to begin hostilities the better he would like it. He wanted this job completed as soon as possible, then he would be able to give his full attention to making that horse his own and, hopefully, killing its owner in the process. He walked to another tree and looked down on the farm below.

They were hidden in the same stand of trees that had been used as a lookout point by Jonas Petterfield and Dick Garde's son two nights earlier. From here he could see someone moving about in the yard, moving between a small animal enclosure and a barn. It only required a few moments observation to know that the activity undertaken by the slight figure he was watching had nothing to do with packing up belongings in preparation for departure. The people on this farm were staying put and that probably meant that the other families were, too. That satisfied Jarvis Wilson: it proffered the opportunity to impose his own tyranny upon them. They would be anxious to get out of the territory when his guns began to blaze, but by then it would be too late. It would be as easy as shooting ducks on a pond.

'Think I'll ride down there and tell them that their time is up and that they need to be gone before the sun goes down.'

'We were told just to watch then report back,' said Gatt, who wasn't yet keen to get back on his horse.

'You watch,' said Wilson, 'I'm tired of waiting.'

Gatt was thinking of his money and didn't want to give Gus Remarque any other cause to withhold it. The rancher had been clear about their task and adamant that they shouldn't make contact with the farmers, but Wilson was already setting his foot in a stirrup and wouldn't be swayed by any argument that Gatt could offer. At that moment, however, the wounded man saw movement on the trail to the north. 'Someone's coming,' he said.

The wagon was bumping over a high mound still about half a mile from the copse where the pair was watching.

'Well,' said Wilson, his tone betraying an edge of amusement, 'Mr Remarque can't hold it against us if we encounter one of the farmers on the trail.' There was a flash of triumph in the look he threw at Gatt. 'Can he?' Then he put spurs to his horse and was heading off in the direction of the oncoming vehicle.

At first, Wilson had directed his mount towards the trail above, on a line that would intercept the route of the wagon, but he hadn't gone far before he realized that the driver had changed course and was making a beeline for the farm below. A confrontation with the wagon driver would now occur in full view of anyone watching from the Skivver place. Wilson wasn't troubled by that thought; in fact he relished the alarm he was likely to cause by a demonstration of violence. Another incident would surely hasten the departure of the dirt grubbers and bring the matter to a speedy end.

During the months they'd been in the area, the settlers had developed a relay system for passing messages from farm to farm. Frank Faulds, being the Skivver family's nearest neighbour, was the usual bearer of information to them from the more outlying homes. He was en route this day to tell Drew Skivver that Dick Garde, Jonas Petterfield and others were planning to drive into Pecos the following day for provisions. This was in accordance with the agreement that had been made at the meeting that had been held a couple of nights earlier. The trip to town had come earlier than Frank had anticipated, but if others were in need of supplies it seemed sensible to go along with them and replenish his own stock.

It was a short journey from his own farm to the Skivvers' place so he'd brought his young sons along for the ride. He was listening to their chatter in the back of the wagon when he saw the rider leave the cover of the small stand of trees and set his animal on a line that would reach him before he got to Drew Skivver's gate. Instinctively, he knew that the oncoming horseman had no friendly intent, and his concern increased when he recognized the long, lean figure of Jarvis Wilson.

Frank considered gathering up his rifle from beneath his feet to counteract any threat that Wilson had in mind, but he didn't. He glanced over his shoulder at his sons, who were playing a game they'd devised with an old sack they'd found tucked under the high seat. Any risk of gunplay would put them in danger. Even if he was forced to eat humble pie, their presence ought to be sufficient to deter Wilson from any act of violence. He swung the team so that it swerved away from a direct meeting with the oncoming rider. He was close to the fence that marked the boundary of Drew Skivver's farm and hoped to reach the gate that was now less than four hundred yards away. Wilson, too, changed course and stopped, broadside on, forcing Frank to haul hard on the leathers and bring his wagon to a halt. The boys tumbled on the flat boards behind, giggling at the event.

'Where do you think you're going?' Wilson's question was asked in a menacing tone that spelt out his intention to disregard the presence of the boys.

Their safety was uppermost in Frank's mind but he was further dismayed by the appearance of another rider. Once more his thoughts strayed to the rifle that was pinned to the floor by his right foot, but once more he made no move to reach for it. 'Visiting.'

Wilson scoffed. 'You've got no time for visiting,' he said. 'You need to go home, load your possessions on this wagon and be out of this country before morning.'

'I'm not going anywhere,' Frank replied, keeping his voice firm.

'You're leaving even if I have to drag you out of here on the end of a rope.' Jarvis Wilson let his gaze settle on the young boys, relaying the message that he would be happy to humiliate Frank in front of his sons. He reached out and grabbed the bridle of the nearest horse and began to lead it in a circle, pointing it back to the northern trail.

Frank Faulds pulled the reins, let the team know that he was still in command and shouted resistance at Jarvis Wilson.

Gatt Stone, too, was shouting as he drew closer. 'Leave it,' he told Wilson. 'Someone's coming.' He pointed back to the hillside beyond the small stand of trees.

Meanwhile, across the fence, another person had become aware of the situation that was developing close to her home. Lottie Skivver had watched the wagon descending from the trail and had witnessed the unconventional manner in which its progress had been arrested by the horseman. At first, with hesitation, curiosity had drawn her towards the scene, but now, still two hundred yards from the action, she was running, her unheard shouts demanding to know what was happening.

Jarvis Wilson had released his hold on the team and had uncoiled the rope that he carried looped over the saddle horn. Gatt Stone's alarm call had had no immediate effect on him – the arrival of another farmer to bully would suit his purpose – but there was no guarantee that the newcomer was one of the settlers. Although he had no qualms about killing the farmer or his offspring it wouldn't pay to do it in front of an independent witness. Such an act could turn squeamish neutrals against the cattlemen's cause, which would displease Gus Remarque. But the farmer had to pay for his defiance; he couldn't allow him to think he'd emerged as the victor of this encounter. Wilson's rope flipped forward and settled over the other man's shoulders. When he spurred his horse, Frank Faulds was jerked forward, his head collided with the solid haunch of one of his horses before his whole body thumped heavily onto the dry rough ground.

Instantly, he was dragged along behind Wilson's horse, his clothes and body ripped and scraped by the multitude of sharp stones that were embedded in the ground. He was pulled in a wide circle and released, bloodied, bruised and barely conscious against the front wheel of his wagon. Wide-eyed, the two boys looked down at their battered father.

Wilson shook his rope free from his victim then drew his revolver. 'Remember,' he told Frank, 'gone by tomorrow, otherwise,' he pointed the gun, 'pop.' Then he raised it so that it pointed at the boys. 'Pop,

pop.' Then he rode away with Gatt Stone following.

If Wilson had known that the person Gatt had seen approaching the farm was Ben Joyner, he wouldn't have been so lenient. If killing the Faulds attracted Ben to within range of his guns, Wilson would have done it with relish. Despite the lack of success so far in their encounters, Wilson had never lost the certainty that he was the better gunman and that the next time they met he would kill the man and take the horse. However, Wilson had no reason to suppose that Ben Joyner had business with the settlers so there was no sign of him or his companion by the time Ben reached the Skivver farm.

Ben's attention was immediately caught by the group of people around the stationary wagon off to his left. When he recognized Lottie as one of the figures kneeling in the dust, he spurred his horse to quickly join them.

They got Frank Faulds into the house where Lottie and her mother worked on him, applying balms and salves to heal cuts and ease swellings. Silently, the boys ate biscuits and drank milk while watching the ministrations to their father. Ben and Drew listened to the details and both were aware that if Wilson had gone through with the killings, Lottie, too, would have been a victim.

'Dick Garde and Jonas need supplies,' Frank told Drew. 'The other night we agreed we'd all go into Pecos together. I came to see if you needed anything.'

'When are you going?'

'Tomorrow.'

'Do you still mean to go?' asked Ben.

The look he cast at the boys carried an unmistakeable meaning but Frank's response cast aside any doubts that the recent event had dented his determination to stay along the Pecos. 'There are things we need.'

Drew Skivver spoke to his wife. 'Sarah, prepare a list and I'll go with them.'

'I'll ride into town with you,' Ben said.

Drew Skivver turned a severe eye on the younger man. 'I might be injured but I still mean to stand alongside my neighbours.'

'Sure,' said Ben. 'I just meant to add to the party.' But he wasn't sure that Drew's presence would be a benefit to the rest of the farmers. One-handed, it was unlikely he'd be able to drive his own team or load anything but the smallest items onto the wagon. 'Let's get there early,' he said, 'before the town's fully awake.'

ELEVEN

Because of a damaged shaft on Dick Garde's wagon, the arrival next morning of the farmers at the Skivver place was an hour later than had been planned. In addition to the Gardes' slow moving vehicle, there were three other wagons, each with at least two men on the driving board. Every family was represented but those whose needs in Pecos were small had agreed to share wagon space. They were accompanied by four mounted men, who were spaced along the flanks like military outriders, but they rode with the awkwardness of those unaccustomed to the saddle. Working the land had made them strong but it was difficult to believe they would be effectivc as a fighting force. The small caravan halted on the trail above Drew Skivver's place and waited for his wagon to join them.

Drew was sitting behind the team but it was Lottie who was handling the leathers. Determined though her father was to ride into Pecos with his neighbours, it was apparent that the physical demands were still beyond his capability. He'd argued against Lottie driving the wagon, worried for her safety when they reached Pecos, but she'd been adamant. Ben Joyner had shared Drew's misgivings and the look he flashed at Lottie when she climbed on to the high board left her in no doubt that he opposed her action. She'd tilted her chin at him as though ready to fight him over the issue so, silently, he'd climbed onto the chestnut and ridden up the hill behind the wagon.

The scheme to reach Pecos, conduct business and be homeward bound before the town was immersed in the full thrust of daily toil had been thwarted by the slow pace invoked by the broken wagon shaft. The streets of Pecos were now alive with regular morning activity. The line of wagons attracted little attention as they filed over the bridge, wound their way between the Mexican buildings and entered Austin Street.

It was customary to load wagons that arrived at the Bartlett brothers' store in the long side alley that ran from Austin Street through to the parallel River Road. The arrival of five in convoy, however, took the storekeepers by surprise, more so when they identified the drivers. The treatment of the farmers by the cowmen was a major talking point and the sight of Drew Skivver with his arm in a sling was a reminder of the recent violence that had occurred only yards from their establishment. The battered face of Frank Faulds was unexpected and the assembly of so many farmers rang warning bells in John Bartlett's mind that a showdown with the cattlemen was the purpose of their visit. The production of lists from shirt pockets, however, lifted his apprehension and the promise of money put a smile on his face that, even if laced with nervousness, was still genuine. So far their arrival in town had not caused a ruckus and if he could attend to them quickly they might be on the road home before news of their visit reached the ears of any cattleman. Accordingly, he left the task of attending to the daily needs of the townspeople to his younger brother and his wife while he filled the orders that were being placed on the counter.

Hitching the chestnut to a rail at the front of the store, Ben Joyner leant against a boardwalk post. When their order was filled, he would help Lottie and her father load the wagon for the return journey but, at present, was content to watch the late morning activity on the street. Although he had no reason to expect an assembly of cowboys in town so early in the day, he was still wary of Gus Remarque's intentions. He remained watchful for people who showed an excessive interest in the farmer's wagons, people who might have sympathy with the cattlemen's cause or the cattlemen's money in their pocket. A quarter of an hour passed before his eyes settled on John Vasey.

The sheriff was sauntering along the street offering greetings to most of the people he met, stopping occasionally in doorways to exchange words with the shopkeeper within. His expression lost much of its cheerfulness when he reached Ben and became aware of the activity in the side alley.

'Don't want you or these people lingering in town,' he told Ben.

'These people are buying supplies. Reckon they'll stay as long as it takes. I'll go when they go.'

'I don't want any trouble.'

'Nor do the farmers. They aren't trying to drive anyone out of their homes.'

John Vasey turned his head, throwing a look towards the hotel that dominated the street. 'Mr Remarque is in town. Stayed overnight at the Alamo.'

'Not my concern,' Ben told the sheriff, but it was news that justified his caution.

'He wants you and Mrs Tippett out of Pecos. The twenty-four hours he gave you is almost up.'

Despite the brusqueness of their confrontation the previous day, the rancher's demand took Ben by surprise. Perhaps, he mused, his former boss had been convinced by Wilson or Davey Pursur that he'd thrown in his lot with the farmers. If that was true, the order merely made it clear that he would be treated in the same manner as his allies. But the inclusion of Mrs Tippett was significant. It meant that Gus Remarque knew who she was, that he was responsible for the deaths of her son and brother.

The sound of horsemen distracted him from his thoughts and both he and the sheriff turned to inspect the new arrivals in town.

Hector Carter wasn't much beyond thirty years of age but he ran one of the larger northern cattle ranches. He'd inherited it from his father who'd settled in the area shortly after Gus Remarque arrived in this part of Texas. Alongside Hector rode another cattle rancher, Tom Wainwright. Each man was accompanied by his top hand, who rode behind. They glanced at the sheriff as they passed, acknowledging him with brisk head movements, but the collection of wagons in the alley didn't escape their attention. Nor did they fail to identify the farmers who were loading those wagons, some of whom ceased their labour to follow the progress of the armed cattlemen as they rode along the street.

'What's going on?' muttered John Vasey. If the question was aimed at Ben Joyner then he had little hope of an answer, but the appearance of Gus Remarque on the veranda of the Alamo Hotel made it clear that a meeting was about to be convened of the main ranchers along the Pecos. In verification, another rancher, Oscar Johnson, arrived in town at some pace, as though he'd been making a determined effort to catch up with the men ahead. As they dismounted outside the hotel, Sheriff Vasey stepped down from the boardwalk, took a few steps in that direction then paused when he came under Gus Remarque's inspection.

The rancher's gaze lifted from the lawman to scrutinize the man with whom he'd been in conversation. He watched as Ben Joyner pushed himself away from the post against which he'd been leaning and returned his stare, refuting the power he had had as employer. As though to emphasise Ben Joyner's opposition, three men, farmers, appeared at his side.

Gus Remarque had never exchanged a word with any of them but he knew the names of Dick Garde, Jonas Petterfield and Frank Faulds. For Gus, their presence in Pecos was an open challenge to his authority. Any words of greeting he intended for his fellow ranchers were forgotten; the purpose for summoning them superseded manners.

'My patience is at an end,' he told them. 'Allowing these land grabbers to build homes and fences only encourages others to do the same. If we let them stay we'll be overrun with farmers stealing our grass. They've killed one of my riders and I want them gone from the river valley today by whatever means is necessary.'

Tom Wainwright rubbed his jaw. He was still doubtful that violence would achieve Gus Remarque's hoped-for results. In his opinion, the killing of the Dutchman had been an unnecessarily brutal affair and Col Brodie's subsequent death a matter of justice rather than a cause for retribution. 'Let's talk about this inside,' he said, pointing the way to the hotel. 'I need a beer to wash the dust from my throat.'

Hector Carter agreed and moved towards the door but it opened before he reached it and he stepped aside to allow the solitary woman to exit. The smile she offered him disappeared when she found herself confronted by Gus Remarque.

'I hope your luggage is packed,' he said bluntly to Elsa Tippett.

'Why would it be?'

'Because I want you out of Pecos along with all the other farmers and land stealers.'

Tom Wainwright found it difficult to hide his anger over Gus Remarque's ungracious remarks. Whatever his cause, this was neither the time nor the place to address the woman with such virulence. It was tantamount to drawing all of the ranchers to his cause, convincing the woman that they were all in accord with Remarque's ultimatum. It wasn't true, that was a personal matter, but the conflict against the farmers, too, was almost a personal matter that Gus Remarque was determined to drag them into. He would have offered some kind of apology to Elsa Tippett on his own behalf but she'd turned on her heel and gone back into the hotel.

Although they were unable to hear his words, his gesticulations made it clear to those watching from the veranda of the general store that Gus Remarque was angry and that they were the objects of his ire. Leaving the farmers on the boardwalk, Ben Joyner left the veranda and joined the sheriff on the road. Side by side they walked towards the hotel. Even though he had no intention of acceding to the order, Ben wanted to know Gus Remarque's reason for wanting him to leave Pecos. He guessed that the short conversation with Elsa Tippett had been on the same subject.

'Mr Remarque,' he called and his challenge gained the attention of all the cattlemen.

Gus Remarque stationed himself at the head of the steps, adopting an aggressive pose, making it clear that there was no place on the hotel veranda for Ben or the sheriff. He looked down on the pair who had stopped at the foot of the five-step flight. With the backing of the most influential men in the area, he was ready for a fight.

All along the street, people had paused, their curiosity pricked by the arrival of the owners of the biggest cattle ranches and further excited by the purposeful manner in which the sheriff made his way up the centre of the road towards the Alamo Hotel. One or two who had been in the vicinity of the general store had seen the assembly of farmers and were now gossiping to their neighbours that the dispute was building to a climax. The killing wouldn't be restricted to those who had already fallen, they prophesised; the situation was building up to a showdown when more blood would be shed. The faint-hearted should get off the street and run for cover.

Gus Remarque brushed aside his jacket so that he could hook his thumbs into the top of his pants. It was an action that showed he wasn't wearing a gun belt. When he spoke, he addressed John Vasey, barely sparing a glance for Ben Joyner as though his former employee was beneath consideration.

'You didn't pass on my instruction to the Tippett woman, Sheriff.'

'No, I didn't.'

Gus Remarque jutted his chin in Ben's direction. 'What about him?'

'I'm in front of you,' Ben said. 'Why don't you

deliver your own message?'

'OK. You've got two hours to get out of Pecos, and this time don't come back.'

'You've got some reason why I shouldn't be here?'

'This is cattle country. There's no room for farmers or turncoats.'

'Mrs Tippett is neither of those. Why do you want her to leave?'

'She came here with you. She leaves with you.'

John Vasey interrupted. 'You don't decide who stays in this town, Mr Remarque. That's my job.'

'Then do it.'

'And you don't have the authority to tell me what to do.'

Gus Remarque raised his eyes from the faces of the men below him and looked over their heads at the movement that had caught his attention. He smiled. 'I think I do,' he said.

The sheriff and Ben Joyner turned as they caught the sound of approaching horses. Instantly, Ben rued the delay caused by the damaged wagon shaft. Without it, the farmers would by now have finished their business and be on the homeward trail. The incoming riders were a bunch from the Long-R led by Davey Pursur. Coming abreast of the general store, the Long-R foreman slowed his pace and made it clear to those loading wagons that they were under his observation, but the group didn't halt there. They continued up the street until they were within a few yards of the hotel, and formed a line that entrapped the sheriff and Ben between themselves and the cattlemen on the veranda. Jarvis Wilson rode his horse alongside Davey Pursur, and Gatt Stone joined them. Marty Levin was one of the four Long-R ranch hands that were a horse length behind.

'Don't try taking matters into your own hand, Mr Remarque,' John Vasey said. 'I told you yesterday that I intended to involve the Rangers and that wasn't an idle threat.'

Talk of the Texas Rangers had an effect on Hector Carter, Tom Wainwright and Oscar Johnson. They exchanged looks that expressed their reluctance to become embroiled in any affair that would put them at loggerheads with the state's lawmen.

'Don't let him bluff you,' Gus Remarque said when he saw their reaction. 'He hasn't sent any messages to Fort Worth or Austin. That would be an admission that he can't keep order in his own town. He's too proud to seek help from state authorities. There are no Rangers on the way to Pecos.'

Gus Remarque's reassurance was less convincing than he'd hoped. His fellow ranchers showed no inclination to back any play he might be considering. In a show of bravado, John Vasey insisted that he didn't want any gunplay between cattlemen and farmers, and that he wanted the guns of the Long-R riders deposited in his office while they remained in town.

It was Jarvis Wilson, of course, who scoffed at the suggestion. 'My gun stays tied to my hip,' he announced.

'Then get out of town,' John Vasey told him.

'Is that what you want, Mr Remarque?'

'No,' said the ranch owner. 'It's those people I want out of town and out of the territory.'

Gus Remarque's comment had been aimed at the farmers who had congregated outside the store. News of the arrival of the cattlemen had put a temporary halt to their dealings with the Bartlett brothers. Now, a couple of them were making their way along the street. Jonas Petterfield was carrying a shotgun and Dick Garde a single shot rifle.

'Looks like they want a fight,' he added.

Ben pushed his way past the cowboy's horses. Like the sheriff, he didn't want the matter developing into a battle. The farmers, he believed, had little chance of emerging as victors if the conflict developed into outright warfare. He could see Lottie and her father anxiously watching the progress of their armed neighbours who were midway between the store and the hotel.

'Stop there,' Ben shouted, holding up his right hand to back up his words.

Behind him, Jarvis Wilson spoke, his voice full of scorn. 'Let them come,' and Ben felt the mounted man's boot full on his back. He was hurtled forward onto the hard, dry street.

Then, amid the shouts of men and the startled cries of horses, the guns began to fire.

Sprawled and face down on the ground, Ben had to twist awkwardly to take in the scene behind. Even as he'd been thrust forward, Ben had heard John Vasey's voice raised in protest, warning everyone that he would have no violence on the streets of Pecos, but the first gunshot cut short his words. Now he was twisting and falling, a gout of blood bursting out of his back to stain the ground where he fell. Ben wasn't sure who had shot the sheriff: Gatt Stone and Davey Pursur were the likely candidates but there was nothing Ben could do to help the stricken lawman. In fact, his own safety was under threat. In response to the urgent calls of Gus Remarque, Jarvis Wilson was reaching for his pistol. There was little doubt he would use it before Ben was able to draw his own gun.

Jarvis Wilson was pulling the reins with his left hand, endeavouring to turn his mount into a position that would enable him to get a clearer shot at Ben. The startled horse reacted clumsily, shaking its head and shuffling its feet in an indeterminate attempt to obey its rider's instructions. Wilson yelled angrily at his mount as he pulled his Colt from its holster but the horse's improper reaction was no longer entirely due to its own failings. Another horse had been ridden into it, the collision so forceful that it had slewed to the right, its back legs folding until it almost sat on the ground.

The rider of the second horse was Marty Levin. 'Get out of here, Ben,' he shouted while making sure that his own horse remained a barrier between Gus Remarque's hired gun and the man on the ground.

From along the street the roar of the shotgun added to the commotion closer at hand. The distance that separated the farmers from the cowboys probably made that weapon ineffective, but nonetheless, it announced their participation in the conflict. Ben wanted to put an end to their involvement, but the safety of Jonas Petterfield and Dick Garde was no less tenuous than his own. Marty Levin's words were still ringing in his ears and he scrambled to his feet and made a dash for the far side of the street.

A gunshot sounded, a man grunted but Ben didn't stop or look back until he reached the temporary sanctuary of the corner of the hardware store. Those who had been drawn by the prospect of an argument between their sheriff and the major surrounding landowners were now scattering as guns were fired and men lay bleeding in the street. Marty was on the ground, lying under the legs of his own horse, his face twisted with agony.

Jarvis Wilson couldn't comprehend the behaviour of Gus Remarque's ranch hand. Ben Joyner would be dead and the big chestnut his if the horse under him hadn't been barged aside. But the older man would pay for his interference. The first shot hadn't killed him but the next one would. However, just as it had done when Ben had been his intended victim, his recalcitrant horse was, once again, making it difficult for him to get a clear line of fire at his target. Then the discharge of the shotgun's second barrel distracted him and he turned his attention to the men firing from further down the street. The farmers were the prime reason he'd come to Pecos; he would return and finish off the wounded Long-R man when he'd dealt with them. He fired his pistol in their direction with little expectation of hitting anyone. He hoped the farmers would run, thereby giving him the pleasure of riding them down. It would be like hunting slow moving game.

After discharging both barrels, Jonas Petterfield cast aside the shotgun and pulled a handgun from the waistband of his trousers. In these later years of his life he'd hoped to live peacefully tilling the land and raising crops, but as a young man he'd been one of Sam Houston's Texas army that routed Santa Anna's Mexicans at San Jacinto. He knew how to fight. Beside him, Dick Garde, who had been a soldier during the Civil War, sighted along the long barrel of the rifle in his hands. He pulled the trigger. Through the rising smoke he saw Davey Pursur throw up his hands as the bullet struck his body. The foreman tumbled from his horse.

That rifle shot surprised Jarvis Wilson, too. It passed so close to his own body that he felt the disturbed air on his cheek. Instinctively, he pulled the reins, roughly, suddenly checking the pace of the mount that, only moments earlier, he'd spurred for pace. The horse, already unnerved by warlike sounds, reared and tumbled, spilling its rider onto the street not far from the corner of the hardware store where Ben Joyner was watching.

Stepping forward, gun in hand, Ben shouted for Wilson to surrender. It was to no avail. Wilson had clung on to his pistol when falling from his horse and was pulling the trigger even as he rose to his feet. He had never had any doubt that he was the better man with a gun so when Ben's bullets smacked into his stomach and he found himself on his knees he could only watch as blood spread across his shirt. Strength left his arms and his pistol fell from his grip. He tried to speak as Ben approached but no words came and he pitched forward on to his face, dead.

Gatt Stone had seen Ben emerge from the side of the hardware building and once again he was overcome with a thirst for revenge. Like Jarvis Wilson, he had never entertained any thought that Ben Joyner would prove to be the better man in a shootout, but he needed to gain his own retribution for the damage that had been done to his shoulder, the pain he still suffered and the humiliation he'd been subjected to by an employer who was reluctant to pay the fee for a task he was barely capable of undertaking. The injury rendered him incapable of drawing a gun with his right hand and his accuracy with his left was not a talent about which he could brag. So, as shots were being exchanged between Wilson and Ben, he dug his spurs into his horse's flanks, aiming it like a missile at Ben Joyner.

A shout from an unrecognized source alerted Ben to the new danger. Even so, he barely had time to react. He jumped backwards but couldn't fully evade the onrushing animal. He was lifted off his feet by the force of the impact and flung heavily on to the ground. His gun was sent flying from his hand in an unknown direction. When he got to his feet, the horse was bearing down on him again. He knew that if he went down under its hoofs it would be the end of him; Gatt Stone was in no mood for showing mercy. A shout of encouragement for his opponent reached his ears. He knew it emanated from Gus Remarque.

The horse hit him again, flinging him into the centre of the street. His head bounced off the road but, although stunned, he knew he had to get up again. The fact that Gatt Stone hadn't used his gun planted the thought in Ben's mind that Gatt's right arm was almost beyond use. It gave him an opportunity for success. In ungainly fashion, he stood and watched as Gatt circled his horse to renew the attack. When it came, Ben dipped his shoulder as though he meant to move to the left side of the horse. Gatt turned his horse, following the line that Ben seemed intent upon. Although groggy and bruised from the buffeting, Ben was still more agile than the horse. At the last moment, he changed direction so that he was at the other side of the horse. Reaching up, he grabbed Gatt's right arm and pulled.

The first squeal of pain confirmed Ben's suspicions: Gatt was handicapped by his injury. As Gatt slid off the side of the horse Ben was able to grab the shoulder. The other man hollered, reflecting the intensity of pain he was suffering. When he hit the ground, Ben stamped on his enemy's injury then thumped his head repeatedly on the hard street until he lost consciousness.

Stepping away from his beaten foe, Ben found himself facing his former employer. At the start of the conflict, Gus Remarque had considered himself certain of victory. The shooting of Sheriff Vasey had been a message to every Pecos citizen that he, Gus Remarque, controlled events in this part of Texas. It should have been the signal for his men to clear every farmer out of the area, but nothing had gone according to plan after that. Marty Levin had openly betrayed him, had prevented Wilson killing Ben Joyner, and the rest of his ranch hands had done nothing to assist. The ranchers too, who had as much to lose from the arrival of land grabbers, had stepped away from him when John Vasey had gone down. Weak men, he thought, who shied from deeds that needed doing and the prospect of a visit from Texas Rangers.

'Well,' he said aloud, 'if I have to do it myself, it merely increases my power.'

Reaching inside his jacket, he produced a Colt from a shoulder holster and pointed it at Ben Joyner. Ben, exhausted and sore, could only look at the hole from which the bullet would come that would end his life. A shot rang out and Gus Remarque stumbled forward, fell to his knees, tried to rise then rolled onto his back. His eyes were open, his lips moving as though he had questions that needed answering.

Ben raised his eyes to the veranda outside the Alamo Hotel. Elsa Tippett still held the rifle tight against her shoulder and she kept it there when she began walking towards her fallen victim. When she reached the place where he lay she looked down on him and it seemed to Ben that she was satisfied that he was still alive.

'You killed my son and my brother,' she said. 'Called them cattle thieves, tied ropes around their necks and choked the life out of them. Cast them aside with the same disdain that you showed for this piece of paper.' From a pocket she'd produced a creased document, which she fluttered in front of his dying eyes. 'But Brad Raine retrieved it, knew it was a legal document for the land you found them on and brought it to me. I came to Pecos to kill you, Mr Remarque. I want you to know that.'

Elsa Tippett pointed the rifle at the rancher's body and pulled the trigger.

For a handful of seconds, silence settled over Austin Street until the doctor darted forward to examine the shot men for signs of life. Then the farmers hurried along the street in the knowledge that their homes were safe, and Lottie Skivver clung to Ben Joyner's arm as though afraid he was about to fall through a hole to the earth's core.

Elsa Tippett shouldered her rifle and returned to the hotel.